OTTO PENZLER PRESENTS
AMERICAN MYSTERY CLASSICS

THE CHOCOLATE COBWEB

CHARLOTTE ARMSTRONG (1905-1969) was an Edgar Award-winning American author of mystery short stories and novels, and a pioneer of the domestic suspense genre. Several of her books were made into films, including *Mischief* (which became *Don't Bother to Knock*), *The Unsuspected*, and *The Chocolate Cobweb*, her fifth novel, which served as the basis for Claude Chabrol's *Merci pour le chocolat*.

A. J. FINN is the author of the #1 *New York Times*-bestselling thriller *The Woman in the Window*, translated into more than forty languages and adapted for the screen as a major motion picture starring Amy Adams, Gary Oldman, and Julianne Moore. A native of New York, Finn worked as a book editor in both England and the United States before turning to fiction.

THE CHOCOLATE COBWEB

CHARLOTTE ARMSTRONG

Introduction by
**A.J.
FINN**

**AMERICAN
MYSTERY
CLASSICS**

*Penzler Publishers
New York*

Published in 2020 by Penzler Publishers
58 Warren Street, New York, NY 10007
penzlerpublishers.com

Distributed by W. W. Norton

Cover image: Andy Ross
Cover design: Mauricio Diaz

Paperback ISBN 978-1-61316-167-8
Hardcover ISBN 978-1-61316-166-1

Library of Congress Control Number: 2020902243

Printed in the United States of America

9 8 7 6 5 4 3 2 1

THE CHOCOLATE
COBWEB

INTRODUCTION

The Chocolate Cobweb is godawful.

Not (I hasten to add) Charlotte Armstrong's novel, first published in 1948 and reissued, more than seventy years later, in the handsome volume you now hold. No—the *title The Chocolate Cobweb* is godawful.

What a hopelessly mismatched pair of nouns! As mutually ill-suited as Oedipus and Jocasta, as Burton and Taylor, as Henry VIII and a quintet of wives. Chocolate: solid or syrupy, depending, but structurally indelicate either way, and altogether common. Cobweb: an elegant trap, an inescapable maze, gossamer-fine yet sturdily built.

Armstrong's novel is just such a marvel, once you turn the title page. Set in late-1940s Los Angeles—the same era, and the same city, as Raymond Chandler's fifth Philip Marlowe case, *The Lady in the Lake* (1949), as well as Dorothy B. Hughes' psychothriller *In a Lonely Place* (1947)—*Cobweb* boasts a canny design, as our heroine, an aspiring artist alternately referred to (by both other characters and the omniscient narrator) and Amanda and Mandy, enmeshes herself in the lives—and installs herself in the home ("cold angles, too much glass")—of the Garrisons, with whom she shares a singular history. Danger stalks this family, rounding those angles, peering through that glass; one of them is marked for death. Until Mandy devises a plan: she'll convince the killer that the victim ought to be . . . the houseguest herself.

Armstrong charges out of the gate. Within the first seven chapters—barely a quarter of the entire text!—she spotlights (a) an intriguing many-moons-ago tale of mistaken identity; (b) the murderer's name; (c) the murderer's method of choice; (d) the intricate solution to a past crime; (e) the results of a critical laboratory test; (f) the mesmerizing portrait of a dead woman; (g) a do-or-die display of uncanny mimicry. (Not necessarily in that order.) Most novelists would reserve these surprises for the home stretch—especially today, when so many (so very, very many) mysteries laze half-comatose for hundreds of pages, only to jolt awake in the final chapter. But Armstrong's Act I signals to us that she has blueprinted her own web, carefully attached each filament of plot to the next, tested the tensile strength of her netting.

And what bright netting it is, too. Grit and grime spackled much postwar mystery fiction: the Chandler and Hughes books noted above, for instance, inhabit a hard-bitten L.A. steeped in violence, disillusionment, and anomie, where dreams die before dreamers do. Armstrong's city, however, basks beneath the California sun; its characters dwell in backyarded suburban homes and glossy, glassy triplexes crouching above canyons; they wear sandals and pumps, pantsuits and sunglasses, all lovingly detailed by Armstrong, who worked in fashion journalism prior to writing novels. (Her magazine's name, *Breath of the Avenue*, nearly rivals *The Chocolate Cobweb* for sheer dissonance.)

These women and men—among them a celebrated actress and a famed painter, both unapologetically wealthy, both wholly sympathetic—seem to *enjoy* life. What a tonic for the reader accustomed to glummer company, to bleaker locales, to more pitiable victims. Armstrong has landscaped an Eden, innocent and wholesome (the second World War is scarcely mentioned); but just as evil slithered into that original nudist colony, a serpent flows through the Garrison house

On the surface, at least, the novel is as fresh-scrubbed as its heroine. Interestingly—almost uniquely in the genre, in my experience—the text refers to her as both Amanda and Mandy by turns, sometimes within successive sentences. It's a shrewd stylistic choice; Armstrong needn't weed out too many instances of one name or the other. (I find this chore deeply boring in my own work.) More than that, though, the name-and-nickname device highlights an essential conflict: Amanda's—and Mandy's—tug-of-war between post-teenage adolescence and womanhood. At twenty-three, she lives happily at home with her mother, longing for an artist's career and uninterested in romance ("I've never been in love in all my life!" she scoffs in Chapter Two). Yet in her quest to solve the riddle of her birth—to find out who she is, genealogically—she also discovers her character, her capabilities, and even her heart. (In one of the novel's most affecting passages, Mandy/Amanda—having come a long way from Chapter Two—informs the man she adores unrequitedly: "'Certainly, I am in love with you. . . . I know how *you* feel. It's O.K.'")

I don't mean to taxonomize here—Mandy isn't necessarily the childish name, nor Amanda the grown-up one. But their double act does suggest to me an identity crisis of sorts in a young woman, lately lounging in her mother's airy living room, now playing cat-and-mouse with somebody smiling at her across an unfamiliar dinner table. The young Miss Garth might remind readers of Nancy Drew—the adventurous spirit and pluck, the comfortable single-parent home, a nighttime reconnaissance mission that finds her scaling the façade of a house barefoot—yet as Armstrong weaves her web, as our self-appointed sleuth climbs its threads like ladder rungs, all the way to the bullseye center, she strengthens and deepens. With her induction into the Garrison household, she can now participate in some of the central rituals of adult life: falling in love, say, or learning one's trade. Or dying.

Armstrong charts this growth with a light touch. Although *The Chocolate Cobweb* ranks amongst the earliest so-called "domestic suspense" novels—a publishing-industry term applied to any book starring an imperiled woman (usually in her twenties or thirties, usually a witless bore) who realizes, albeit not until long after the reader does, that Someone Wants Her Dead—this is a good-humored mystery, agreeably earnest and self-aware in equal measure, written smoothly and peopled sparingly. (So much crime fiction, I've realized of late, seems preposterously overstuffed with characters. Writers in the genre would do well to study *Cobweb*, both for Armstrong's judicious population control and for her plotwork, which distributes weight evenly across the pages.)

Typically, when a mystery features a character who "comes of age," that process feels entirely incidental; the individual in question was immature on page one, but by The End, she or he is all grown up. The events of her adventure have sculpted her into a Woman; having pitched the villain from a roof, he is now a Man. In the latter chapters of *Cobweb*, as our heroine engages in some especially nimble psychological gamesmanship, I realized that, here, it isn't the story that powers the character's growth; it's the character's growth that powers the story. Throughout much of the plot, Amanda's actions are entirely elective. She *chooses* to investigate her origins; she *chooses* to infiltrate the Garrison home; she *chooses* to dare and provoke her enemy. These are adult decisions—some more rash than others, certainly, but generally made with consideration and all available foresight. This is an uncommonly proactive protagonist—a web-weaver, increasingly methodical and ever more subtle.

After death—indeed, very often decades before death—popular authors vanish with alarming frequency, their books forgotten, their legacies reduced to elliptical and broadly inaccurate Internet biographies. To browse bookstore shelves stocked with reissued Golden Age mysteries, or neglected noir classics, or detective series published just ten or twenty years ago, is to marvel at how, even for bestselling novelists, a shelf life of any sort is no guarantee. Charlotte Armstrong, alas, joined the ranks of the lost after her death in 1969, at the age of sixty-four, despite having won an Edgar Award, written two Broadway plays, and seen several of her books adapted for the screen.

The legendary Claude Chabrol directed a French adaptation of *The Chocolate Cobweb*, entitled *Merci pour le chocolat* and starring Isabelle Huppert, in 2000. Other films based on her books were *Don't Bother to Knock* (from her novel *Mischief*, which starred Richard Widmark and Marilyn Monroe); *La Rupture* (also directed by Chabrol, adapted from *The Balloon Man*); *The*

Unsuspected (from the book of the same title—also published in the American Mystery Classics series—the Michael Curtiz noir classic starring Claude Raines and Audrey Totter); and *The Three Weird Sisters* (from *The Weird Sisters*).

Armstrong left a trove of nearly thirty novels, two of which I pounced on immediately after bidding farewell to the Garrisons and their twice-named protector. I look forward eagerly to reading more—and I'm pleased to report that none of them are burdened with a title as bad as *The Chocolate Cobweb*.

—A. J. FINN
New York, 2020

THE CHOCOLATE
COBWEB

1.

Cousin Edna Fairchild had designed her life on the principle that far fields are greener. During a quarter of each year she flitted about Southern California, visiting a week here, a fortnight there, hinting delicately, among barbarians, of her nostalgia for the riper culture of the eastern seaboard. The rest of the year she dwelt in New York City and basked in some glory as one who wintered on the west coast and could speak wistfully of relaxed and freer customs among those who had escaped toward the sun.

Now, on a March Sunday morning, she was about to make her annual spring leap from west to east. She was going home.

They sat in the patio at the back, among the Sunday papers and the dregs of breakfast. It was that sterile hour before departure. All news had long since been told. Old times had been chewed over and the flavor exhausted. In fact, Cousin Edna was already mentally on the train and Kate Garth, her hostess, had already mentally straightened out Amanda's room and moved Amanda back into it.

Amanda was going to drive the traveler to the station. She didn't look it. She was barefoot and wore a tight pair of tattered and faded blue pants, a rose-colored shirt with the sleeves rolled up. She sprawled on the chaise, leaning on her elbows, studying the newspaper. Her short brown hair curled and clung to her pretty head.

"Mandy," said Cousin Edna, "hadn't you better get dressed?"

"Take me five minutes," said Amanda serenely. "We've got two hours."

Cousin Edna rose, strolled to the edge of the brick-paved patio, and looked around as if to soak up the sight of white walls enclosing the small pleasant yard, stylized blue froth of wisteria bloom, the gray-green olive tree. "Well, Kate, it's been lovely!"

Amanda's blue eyes slid to watch the patience deepen comically on her mother's face. Kate had been driven to mending. She couldn't read under Edna's nose. But her long strong fingers were clumsy with a needle and she took big stitches, like a child.

"What are you studying?" Cousin Edna bent over Amanda's shoulder. "'Belle in the Doorway.' Hmmmm. . . ."

Amanda's gaze flicked back to the half-tone reproduction of a painting, there on the Sunday art page. "It's not a very good picture," she remarked with young scorn, and caught quickly at her own arrogance to qualify it: ". . . in my humble opinion. . . ."

"I was going to say . . ." murmured Kate mildly.

"Still so interested in art," cooed Cousin Edna.

"I think it's a stupid picture." Amanda struck the paper with the backs of her fingers. "The drawing is terrible. The light's unnatural. The subject's sentimental."

"'Tobias Garrison,'" read Cousin Edna. "Garrison! Why, Kate, isn't that the man?"

Amanda's chin tipped. She looked warily at Kate. She read on that long face the tiny reaction of regret and then the gathering of some patience and fortitude to overcome it.

"The artist!" Cousin Edna was insisting. "The same man! The one in the hospital that time! Don't tell me you've forgotten!"

"What time?" said Amanda bluntly.

"Why, the mix-up," said Cousin Edna. "When you were born. I haven't thought of that for years. Isn't it the same man? Isn't it, Kate?"

"I suppose it is." Kate's blue eyes went to Amanda with an odd, flat, bleak courage.

"I'll never forget John Garth that day!" cried Edna. "Never! The way he stood up . . . The way he simply refused to be shaken! I had to admire him. It was such an odd thing. Anybody else might have been upset. Such a new baby, and John himself hardly used to the idea that he had a daughter. I really . . . What's the matter? Oh, Kate, have I said what I shouldn't? Didn't Amanda . . . ? Oh, Kate!" This was a cry but it wasn't quite contrite. There was a bit of relish in it.

In a flash, Amanda chose her side. If there was a secret, it wasn't going to be told now, by Edna, or by Kate in front of Edna, or under Edna's avid eyes, at all. "Oh, *that!*" said she. "Didn't know what you were talking about for a minute." She let herself collapse on one arm, pulled the paper up with the other hand.

"Oh, then you knew? Then I haven't . . . ? Oh. . . . Oh, well, I'm glad!" And Edna sighed a windy disappointed sigh. "But isn't that strange?"

"Not very," said Kate calmly, "since he lives out here."

"Kate, have you ever met him?"

"Never."

"Have you, Mandy?"

"Hummmmm?" said Mandy dreamily. "Nuh-uh. . . . I don't understand all the excitement about this painting."

"My goodness," said Edna, "if you're both so bored . . . ! Why, he's a famous man! Isn't he?"

"It's quarter to . . ." said Mandy.

"Amanda! You're not going like that!"

"Don't you worry about me."

Making anxious sounds, Edna fluttered indoors. The screen slammed. The sharp slap of the wood made a period. Bees buzzed in the sun.

Amanda sat up and turned around, put both bare heels on the brick floor, and curled up her toes. "Oh, boy!" she said. "I've got a mystery about my birth!"

Kate's long clown face began to be convulsed with laughter. Her brows drew up, eyelids made triangles. "I don't know what I'm laughing at," she said. "Oh, me . . . !" But she knew. It was this quick denial of a tiny doubt, denied so absurdly by Amanda's wide-open enthusiasm. So it was the warm certainty, the pure joy of their solidarity. It was a surge of love in Kate's heart for the girl in the outlandish clothes whose faith was so strong that she invited her mother to be excited and amused by the sudden dizzy notion that perhaps they weren't related.

"You'd better tell me," said Amanda, grinning and folding her legs up under her. "If I'm a duchess in disguise I want to know."

Kate shook her head. "There's nothing to it. If I've never told you, it's partly because it's so unimportant, and maybe partly because of that demon imagination. . . ."

"If you think I've outgrown it," said Mandy severely, "I have not."

"Well, all right. The beans are spilled, such as they are." Kate sobered her face. "It seems Mrs. Garrison had a baby just when I did. Same place. Same time. Oh, a few hours' difference. It must have been a little early for her, because Mr. Garrison," she nodded at the paper, "wasn't around. Naturally, he came rushing back from wherever he was and he got to the hospital the next morning. Well, he couldn't see his wife right away, I suppose they were bathing her or something. So he rushed up to the nursery and asked one of the little student nurses to show him his child. And she showed him you."

"For heaven's sake," said Mandy mildly.

"She held you up, behind the glass, of course. She told him you were a girl. And he, naturally, just beamed on you. And then he went in to see his wife and in a little while it turned out that while *he* thought they had a daughter, *she* thought they had a son."

"It came out," commented Mandy, "in the course of conversation, hm?"

Her mother cast her an eyebeam. "So there was an uproar. I really heard very little of it at the time. But it seems he had the nurses tearing around in a panic. And he stirred up all the officials and called all the doctors to come running."

"But how could it happen?"

"That's what he wanted to know. As I understood it. . . . You know they put little bead bracelets on the babies and each bead has a letter on it. The bracelet spells the name. Yours broke. It's unheard of and nobody knew how it could have broken, but it did. So the little student picked up the broken cord with just three beads left on it, the first three letters. . . ."

"Which were G-A-R," said Mandy. "Because they didn't know our first names, did they? Yes. Very neat. Of course, she knew by my pretty face I was a girl."

"She knew," said Kate dryly. "And then your father came."

John Garth was dead, been gone twelve years. Yet, just for a moment, he was alive again. Kate Garth could see him, leaning over the high bed. She heard the quiet quality of his voice.

"He just simply made everybody calm down," she said. "You were our daughter and that was all there was to it, and if there had been some kind of mistake, it was none of our affair, and they'd better straighten it out without upsetting *me*, or it would be our affair and they'd be sorry. He got the doctors and nurses and this Garrison man and held a kind of court of inquiry and really untangled the thing. Your father was . . . very good at that."

Amanda wanted, wildly, to cry. She choked down the sensation. She said, in wonder, "Dad kinda wanted a son, too."

"Not after he saw you."

For a moment, Mandy couldn't see across the space between them. "I must have been pretty attractive when I was young," she sniffled.

Kate swallowed hard herself. "That's all," she said. "So you're no duchess, Duchess." She added dreamily, "*She* must be a nice woman. She wrote me a little note. Though I never saw her."

In a moment or two, Mandy stood up and stretched. "Well, I'm disappointed," she said, yawning. "Mother, how come all this was in New York? I thought you said the Garrisons lived out here. You mean they moved here since, as we did?"

"No," said Kate. "No, I think they were California people, even then. I don't know why they'd come east for the event. I don't know much about them. Oh, I've seen the name. It seems to me there was some tragedy. . . ."

Mandy stood with her arms raised. Kate's face was puzzled, trying to remember. Mandy lowered her arms slowly. She sat down on the chaise and picked up the art page. There was quite an article about Tobias Garrison. Dean of California artists, they called him. The grand old man. An exhibition of his work, currently, at the Peck Galleries. She skimmed the story.

There was no tragedy mentioned. At a banquet, last night, they had given him a plaque. Some Art Association prize. He'd made a speech. Mrs. Garrison was there, in black velvet. Tobias Thone Garrison, the artist's only son, had been expected, but bad flying weather in the East had prevented his arrival in time for the dinner.

Years in the Orient. Return to his canyonside home before the war. Garrison scholarships given . . . The show at the Peck Galleries had been up for two weeks. Included the famous "Belle in the Doorway." Last day today. . . .

Last day today.

"Amanda!" Cousin Edna, with her hat on, was outraged in the house door.

"Belle in the Doorway," thought Amanda. She squealed and fled.

Five minutes later a poised young woman in a soft wool suit, the color of a pale banana, cut on the simplest lines, worn smartly with a dull brown blouse, put a pretty leg, neat in nylon, and a graceful foot in a high-heeled brown pump over the doorstep. This apparition held a brown bag under one arm, car keys in a gloveless hand. She wore no hat, but her hair clung softly like a shining cap, and the sunlight, as she inclined her head, bronzed it a little. She said graciously, "If you are ready, Cousin Edna?"

Cousin Edna, who would never look like that in all her life, bristled with natural resentment, but she kept her stream of compliments and grateful thanks turned on as they all moved toward the alley garage.

"Oh, Mother," said Amanda at the last minute. "You don't want the car this afternoon, do you? I might not come straight home."

"I don't need it. Supper?"

"I'll be home for that. I have a date with Gene, after. You don't mind, Mother?" Blue eyes were confident.

Blue eyes met them and smiled. "No, go ahead," said Kate. She added, "I don't know as I blame you." Because she knew full well where Amanda was going.

2.

Amanda, driving with unconscious skill, blocked and turned aside all Cousin Edna's references to Tobias Garrison. There was a temptation to let go and listen to Edna's account, since she had evidently been on the scene, twenty-three years ago. But Mandy felt that such listening would involve some disloyalty to Kate. Or might tip off Cousin Edna that she had spilled the beans, after all. Amanda stuck stubbornly to indifference.

Once, however, she had given Cousin Edna over to the Pullman Company, she turned the Chevrolet out of the station plaza and went up Sunset, thinking of nothing else. There was no disloyalty in imagining . . . imagining anything. Kate would understand that. Kate would know that no imagining could ever alter the love between them, which existed for its own sake, now and forever.

What if . . . ? Amanda embarked on wild surmise with a smile at herself. What if there really had been a mix-up? What if Kate didn't know all the facts? What if there had been real doubt about whose baby was which? What if it had been settled, arbitrarily, on an uncertain basis, after all? Maybe Kate didn't know that. Maybe she had been spared. Amanda thought vaguely of blood tests. She knew there were such things and she knew a little bit about them. They were negative evidence, at best. Yet Kate hadn't said anything about tests. Of course, probably it hadn't been necessary to go so far. Other evidence had been conclusive. Yet, what if . . . ? What if . . . ?

Well, what?

Tobias Garrison was a famous man, possibly a wealthy man. What would it mean if she were his daughter? Amanda bit her lip. It would mean, she thought, exactly nothing. She didn't know him, had no feeling about him, hadn't been subjected to his influence or his teaching, didn't know what he thought, didn't care. No, no matter what the facts were, she was Kate's daughter and John Garth's daughter. And the fame or wealth of a possible blood parent whom she had never seen, and probably, she told herself, wouldn't even like, meant nothing at all. Her "What if . . . ?" led nowhere. It was a strangely empty dream.

Yet, there was such a thing as heredity. Wasn't there? This yen to paint, this fascinated pull she felt toward the making of pictures . . . A little tendril of excitement crept up her throat. But she went honestly back to a fact. That needn't be explained by heredity. It was already explained, by environment, again, and also Miss Alice Anderson.

As for heredity, it was from John Garth she got her ambition to be a designer. It was from him she took the resolution to study, to go to art school out here. It was from him, by way of his old friend Andrew Callahan, that she got her chance, that she held her part-time job.

John Garth had dealt with the manufacture of printed fabrics. He had never, himself, studied the artistic side of it in any school.

What he knew was self-taught. What he had done, Amanda thought, had been good, but tentative and unsure. She was going further.

Eleven years old she had been when he died, young, of a sudden infection, but she had, even then, been fascinated by color and line. They had played with such things together.

Two years after he died, Kate had decided to come west. The place where he had been was lonely without him. Kate's health had been shaky. And Andrew Callahan had been importunate and kind. Kate worked in the office of Callahan's Sons, Fine Fabrics, Los Angeles. Her strong steady spirit presided firmly over accounts. She was a good businesswoman. Her bedrock dependability was invaluable, Andrew said.

And so, between them, between Andrew, who loved Kate, and Kate, who loved Mandy, Mandy got to go to art school mornings. Afternoons, in an informal and delightful kind of way, she fooled with designing, behind the scenes at Callahan's, where professionals listened to her young ideas with affectionate respect.

I am a lucky girl, thought Mandy solemnly. She would become a designer. She would be a good one, a really good one. She would do exciting things. She would forget, or at least put by as a passing phase, the influence of her teacher, Miss Alice Anderson, whose almost religious reverence for Fine Art, and particularly Fine Painting, was at the bottom of this present passion.

Mandy, scooting up Sunset Boulevard, felt herself become of age, renouncing childish things. Kate, clearheaded Kate, who made plans and stuck to them, had been a trifle uneasy over this tangential interest. Kate, dear, good, wonderful Kate, who left her so free but never freed herself, might, she knew, even marry

Andrew Callahan someday. Someday, when Mandy was settled. When Mandy was out of art school and embarked solidly on her career. Or if Mandy herself were to marry.

She shook her shoulders, impatient with herself suddenly. There was Gene Noyes.

Amanda's pretty figure and the swash and verve of her personality were what made her first impression. Not her face. She had a straight nose, which took a shallow angle, a rather small full mouth, level brows, blue eyes, not large but lovely, and the whole cast of her face was somehow medieval. It might have belonged to a pretty little Italian boy angel in an old painting. Most of her friends would not have called her pretty. Some discerning few would have said she was a beauty.

Gene thought she was beautiful. He was a chemist at Callahan's. He worked with the dyes. He was redheaded, snub-nosed, freckled, and devoted. Amanda admitted to herself, although to no one else, that sooner or later she would probably marry him.

Not now. Not now. Not even now, when she was seeing so clearly the pattern of her life and how its design fell in with the patterns of other lives around her. Not yet.

She would be childish, if that's what it was, for another day, for another afternoon. She would go and look at pictures, and she would wonder about the man who might have been her father, and she would try to understand, and she would snoop at the outskirts of a world that fascinated and drew her, although it was not in the pattern.

Near the Beverly Hills Hotel she turned down toward Wilshire. The Peck Galleries were rather new and very smart.

The doors were translucent glass with a chaste and frosty design. The anteroom was the last word in quiet elegance.

Amanda got herself a catalogue. The rooms were in line and so presented a long, long vista. They were not crowded. Still, rather a surprising number of people stood about, some alone and lost in looking, some whispering to each other.

Tobias Garrison. His date was on the catalogue. He was sixty-five. So old? A life's work, then. Amanda started down the rooms.

Ah, yes, first came the Oriental things. Not Oriental in the sense of the Asiatic mainland. Not Chinese. These pictures came out of the islands. There was nothing radical about the work, or exciting, she thought. Canvases were warm, happy, exuberant, drenched in light and color . . . color . . . color. . . . Yummy, thought Amanda. The man's a colorist. She nodded sagely and admired the things he could do that she could not. The colors splashed and sang. Amanda felt that the artist had been playing . . . playing happily, joyously. But it was not—no, she thought, dissatisfied—not what Miss Alice Anderson had taught her to call Fine Painting.

She passed along to the next room. According to the catalogue, these canvases were of an earlier date. Ah, she thought, feeling very wise, this is the stuff he had to learn first, and then forget, in order to be able to do those others. Here was more form, more care, more sobriety, more conscious control. More mind, less feeling. Color, still, but gentler color. Yes, some of these things were good, really good. Amanda smiled, realizing full well that by this inner comment she meant she liked them. She admired the skill, recognizing it with despair for her own lack. She went all around the room, absorbed, delighted, and then, suddenly, woke up to the fact that she wasn't sure any more. No, no, she was wrong. The first room was better. This was the artist at work, seriously. But those other things, those paintings that almost laughed aloud . . .

Amanda said to herself severely, You don't know a darned thing about it; that's what's the matter.

She drifted into the last room. A group of people had collected, halfway down, all gazing toward the end wall. Amanda didn't push to see what they were looking at. She took the side walls first. Yes, these were the most recent. California, America spoke in the backgrounds. A blend and a summation. Rich color, but not rioting. No laughter. Gentleness, instead. Delicacy. Sometimes sadness.

People moved, murmuring, past her. Now she turned for a free look at the end wall.

Five portraits hung there. But she saw only the one in the center. And down her nerves tingled a shock of pleasure so strong that she turned away to hide it. She swayed, rocking with the impact. She felt no one must know. It was something so intimately touching that it must not be betrayed to a stranger's eye.

Then she focused her eyes and looked carefully at the portraits that flanked the center, two on a side. All four were of a woman, the same woman. A dark-haired, dark-eyed woman with a round face, a gentle, almost sentimentally sweet curve to her chin. These were "good work," all of them. They varied as if the artist had been experimenting. They were "studies." They were dull.

The painting in the center was "Belle in the Doorway."

Amanda turned her head and caught it, sidewise, and caught her breath again. No wonder it was famous! It was a bitter thought, she mused, to have to concede that crowds of other people must receive, as she did, so deep and personal an impression. Mandy shook herself and turned straight toward it.

"Belle" meant no classification of females, as she had half imagined. It was a woman's name, and this woman's name. And this was she. "The drawing's terrible," Mandy had said. But oh, the color! Drawing didn't matter. The woman was alive. "The light's unnatural," Mandy had said. Of course it was unnatural. It radiated from the woman, from the rosy color of her clothes. She was the supernatural source of light. She stood in the doorway and behind her there was a sunny garden. Before her, the dim room, with a few pieces of furniture, one chair, a little shelf, a carpet. And she brought in the light, and the glow of her self, as if she were the sun.

The woman was medium tall and slim, with chestnut hair and brownish eyes, but it wasn't that. It wasn't her body. It was her radiance. "The subject's sentimental," Mandy had said. Now, seeing it before her, she wanted to weep. All right. It's sentimental. It's terrific. It's the dangedest picture I ever saw! She stood with tears stinging her eyelids. A thought walked into her mind, uninvited, unannounced. I've never been in love in all my life! thought Amanda Garth.

Some time later a stir, far behind her, broke the spell. Even before the rushing whispers that ran down the rooms like foam on an incoming wave had reached her ears, Amanda knew that Tobias Garrison himself had just entered the galleries. She clutched at her catalogue and drew away, turning from the experience of this painting, putting it aside to watch, with the rest, the man and woman who were walking slowly down the long way toward her. "Mr. and Mrs. Garrison," somebody said aloud.

It wasn't the woman who interested Amanda. This man, this Tobias, she saw, was rather tall, rather thin, white-haired. He had a weary elegance, a tired distinction. He came slowly along, listening, with politely tilted head, to a young man beside him, and his eyes ran nervously away from the gaze of the spectators. He was not one who listened for inaudible fanfares. He seemed, indeed, to wince away from them.

As he came nearer, Amanda looked at his hands. Oh, good hands, she thought, strong working hands. The thin fingers were restless and nervous on the rolled-up catalogue.

Their group came to a standstill in the center of this third room. Amanda, hovering along the wall, was sorry that Garrison turned his back squarely on the wall of the portraits, so she couldn't study his face. She sidled a little to her right. But it was no use. She could not walk deliberately around to gawk at him, even if others were doing exactly that, and the Garrisons pretended not to mind.

But Mrs. Garrison, she realized, didn't mind. Not at all. Mandy looked at her now. The woman, the mother, hadn't been conspicuous in her imaginings. But after all, this man had to have a wife. The baby in the hospital, twenty-three years ago, had to have a mother.

Mrs. Tobias Garrison was a little woman. She was getting along. She was probably close to sixty, herself. She was plump, not fat, but filled and rounded. Her hair was abundant and pure white and done up on top of her head in a style that, like her funny little hat, was either very new or very old-fashioned. On this small, smiling, round-cheeked little person, it was definitely quaint.

Amanda watched her put down her purse and catalogue on the cold stone bench, to lift her small, soft, rosy hands to the fastenings of her wrap. Why, she's cute! thought Mandy. Cute as a button! With those bright button eyes, dark eyes, missing nothing. Puffed up like a little pigeon, she was, proud and pleased. *She* heard the trumpets blowing, clear enough. She preened herself in the glory, this beaming Mrs. Santa Claus in modern dress. In a neat gray frock, a soft gray jacket, white frill at the throat. And then that bonnet, trimmed with violets.

The earnest young man was talking to her. Mandy heard him say, "Must send a catalogue to Leonard. He'll be so *in*tristed!" He looked about him, and reached down.

"That's mine," said Mrs. Garrison.

"Oh, I beg your pardon."

Her catalogue, on the bench. Just a catalogue, like all the rest. Heaps of them in the foyer. The Garrisons must have others. They must have come often. Mandy blinked.

Tobias, turning, said, "Take this one, Dave. Wait, I'll put a note on it. Have you a pen, my dear?"

Small hands worked on the clasp of her gray cloth purse. It opened gingerly. "Don't press, now, Toby."

Tobias took the pen from her and poised to write. His gaze came up into space, as he stood, composing phrases. Amanda now saw his eyes, blue and yet dark, deep-set and sad. Loss, she thought. He's lost something.

She pivoted to look away. No use denying it. She was excited. Curiosity about these people burned like a flame in her mind. The little woman in gray with those dark eyes and that soft round chin was the woman of the portraits. All four other portraits. But she was not Belle. No, not Belle.

"Ione!" said a female voice. "My dear, how nice! Tobias, how are you?"

It was Fanny Austin. That's who it was! Amanda was startled by her own instant recognition. Every line on that aging pug face under the flagrant false brilliance of her auburn hair was deeply and dearly familiar. Fanny Austin could play any but the merely glamorous female and her presence in the cast of a motion picture guaranteed it serious critical attention, gave it A for Art, as it were. This was Fanny Austin, whose bone-deep experience of the stage she'd left behind her, and whose sheer intelligence and skill had made her the dowager queen of Hollywood.

"My pen, please, Toby," said Mrs. Garrison. "How are you, Fanny?"

Amanda moved down the wall, farther away. One couldn't eavesdrop. She sat down, at last, on another of the stone benches that dotted the rooms. She was near the wide arch now and could look back on them. She chose not to look, for a little while, and riffled the pages of her catalogue. She turned sideways, gazing into the middle room.

She saw him come in. She thought, first, What a beautiful head!

Amanda had heard, in her day, a full quota of wolf calls. She was not a young woman the male eye skipped over too lightly. She reacted, now, as what young person can help reacting to a contemporary, especially an attractive contemporary, of the other sex. She expected to be seen. But although the young man who came striding through saw her clearly enough, sitting there in her cream-yellow and brown, looking very smart and pretty too, profile raised, eyes calm, all innocent beauty, his glance crossed hers coolly. He looked, saw, dismissed, and went on.

Amanda turned her head sharply to look after him, and caught in the corner of her eye the unmistakable identical reaction. Another girl, across the way, had stood in innocent beauty, and had been ignored and knew it. Amanda bit her lip. So, she thought. Mows them down, does he? Who is he? Who is that?

She turned squarely around to stare and abandoned all poses. Her lips parted. One might almost say that her pretty mouth fell open.

Tobias Garrison's deep, sad eyes were lit with pure joy. He stepped to the meeting. Hands met. The group opened like a flower. It was father and son! Of course, it was father and son! Tall, wide-shouldered son, dark beautiful head bent . . .

Amanda got up and walked nearer, forgetting all about manners. She saw and felt it. Father and son! The look on the faces. The faint tan on Tobias' thin face seemed to deepen as if the flesh came alive. And the son's face! Her heart turned over. The light, the sweetness of that smile!

"Thone!" cried Fanny Austin, her rich warm voice vibrating with greeting.

"Well, Thone," said the little Mrs. Garrison more sedately.

He put an arm across Fanny's shoulders. He gave Ione his left hand, drew her near with it, and kissed her cheek lightly. And looked again at his father.

Amanda thought, I will go home. She moved back, softly, against the wall. She felt very lonely all of a sudden. But she couldn't go. She saw this Thone swing slowly, looking over the show of pictures on the walls. Saw Tobias step and stand shoulder to shoulder, to swing with him. She saw the two of them turn, at last, to the end wall.

She held her breath. She could see his profile, then his three-quarter face as he turned to the artist. Her thoughts were chaotic. If he felt toward that picture anything like she did, there would be some meaning. . . . But he did not! She read the rueful shake of his head, the puzzled drawing together of those fine brows, as he said, without words, but plain to see, to his father, "No. No, I don't get it." And Tobias was not hurt or disappointed, but rather pleased, for he clapped his hand on the high shoulder and seemed to stand straighter in some secret understanding.

To herself, Amanda Garth said, I will know them. Her blood tingled with the resolution. Not now. Not here. But I will know them. I want very much to know them. She walked slowly back through the galleries. It was a tearing feeling. But I will know them, she thought again. Her chin was up.

She thought, He's twenty-three. His birthday is mine. All her life, so far, Amanda had automatically subscribed to the universal convention that a girl of, say, twenty-three needs a man who is at least twenty-five, and better, twenty-seven. Or even thirty. She was now, suddenly, enlightened. What superstitious nonsense! she thought.

She came out of the glass doors to the street. She didn't seem able to move very fast. She dawdled toward the car.

They were coming out! Her heart jumped.

Smack in front of the door, arrogantly, stood a Lincoln Continental convertible, a handsome thing, a car for young and beautiful people that young and beautiful people almost never could afford. It was for them, of course, that car.

But it was odd. It was really very odd. She watched them get into it. Fanny Austin in the back. Mr. and Mrs. Garrison in the front. Then Thone got into the back with red-haired Fanny. And when the car moved off, softly, sleekly, surely, carrying them away, the hands on the wheel were the little plump hands of the little lady, Ione.

3.

Tobias Garrison said, often, that this canyonside house he lived in was Old-fashioned Modern, which was to say a weird and uncomfortable concoction of half-baked ideas. He said it wasn't pretty and it didn't make sense. But Ione liked it.

In the first place, it was hers. Toby had put it in her name, alone, a few years back, because he knew how this would please her. It was also, she felt, an unusual house, unlike other people's. And it was high. It was above. And if it had flaws, they were, by now, such familiar flaws that they pertained and belonged to her like wrinkles on her own face.

It was a structure of gray stucco and glass with some stone. It crouched like an animal with forepaws on the brink of a precipice, and its body fell off down the chasm. Although it hardly seemed a living thing, with so many cold angles, too much glass. It had not the window eyes, the roof-and-chimney hat, the face of a house at all. If a molten mixture of stucco and glass had spilled there and begun to slide in huge drops over the edge and been arrested and crystallized into cubes, just such a monstrous effect might have resulted.

Since it poured over to the north, the light within was steady, and from most of its glassed openings one saw, looming far over the opposite canyonside, the high mountains. So it did well enough for Tobias, who lived and worked on the topmost level.

Ione didn't mind the stairs. She liked the hanging spaces. She was not sensitive to its ugliness, and anyhow, by now, on the narrow terraces that followed it downhill, the planting and especially the vines had softened and hidden the worst of its bald, preposterous lines.

It was a fine, big house. Also, it was hers.

Ione stood in the kitchen, which looked off west into the green head of the canyon. Dinner over, Elsie was moving in and out of the dining room, with dishes. Elsie was old, taciturn, comfortable, and settled. Life here in the canyon house ran smooth in the harness of routine, and Ione's little hands were firm on the reins.

Except, she thought with a trace of anger, when Thone was here.

Still, one needn't bother with anger. She slipped a teaspoon into the chocolate simmering on the stove to taste and test its temperature. The pills were safe in her left palm with her fingers folded over them.

Thone! What an idiotic name for a boy! Thone, because it was *her* name. Belle's name.

The chocolate was not yet hot enough. "Did you rinse the thermos, Elsie?"

"Yes, ma'am."

He was an odd boy, Belle's son, raised in the Far East, outlandishly. She could hint at this. Her thought wheeled and veered.

Tobias would be prostrated. His grief would have to be shielded, of course. So it would be Ione who could touch and guide their impressions to the firm conclusion, suicide. Yes, if she hurried! No doubt Thone wanted to see his father one last time. . . .

Suicide, of course. It couldn't appear to be anything else. They weren't going to know how *she* felt, any more than they had known last time. And whatever would happen to Thone's money—Belle's money—it could never, never come to Ione. Or even, supposing it came to Tobias, it was silly for anyone to imagine this a motive, because, of course, Toby already had plenty of money, and half of what he had was her by law.

Suicide, then. It was a matter of conceiving clearly the necessary impression. Why, for instance, would a young and fairly wealthy man desire to die? Mother's tragic ending? No, she'd better not touch that. The business of the girl would do. Preying on him . . . sensitive boy. . . . She still had a letter the girl had written. She'd reveal it, reluctantly.

It would work out.

And that, she thought, would be the end of it. Not again would this house, or the knit skein of her memories, the web of her plans, the whole rhythmic fabric be torn and shredded. Not again would she feel the life of the house change and fall from her and disintegrate and form again in a pattern of memories she didn't share. That were not hers at all. But Belle's. Oh, that gash—that torn-out piece—that would not heal over or finally disappear, until tomorrow.

Why, the minute he came, this Thone of *hers*, Tobias slipped away into another world. And it was a world all Belle's. Belle, here in this very house. Her ways. Her methods. No doubt her face, in all these doorways.

Ione thought, I'll even get Toby to sell the picture, as he sold the rest, once this is over. And the one Thone has! That, too, he'll sell. That *will* be all. She *will* be gone. There will be nothing, no one left, no *thing* left, to speak of her.

Except Fanny. Fanny, who could enter either world. Well, Fanny didn't talk when Thone wasn't here. Oh, it was unfortunate that Fanny had come home with them today. Yes, thought Ione, she must be quick and accomplish her plan, this long imagined plan, tonight, immediately. Before Fanny could see and hear enough of Thone to contradict. . . . Because there must be that gently guided suggestion of a suicide motive, a suicide mood, seeping through.

"Mmmmmm, see . . ." she could say, to the police, of course. There would be police, she supposed. A nuisance.

Still, there had been police the other time, too, and it hadn't made any difference. All had gone well.

She would say that Thone asked her for the sleeping medicine. Asked at her door, late, as they went down to bed. This was safe, because Tobias slept above, here on the top floor, while her room and Thone's were one flight down. And alone there. Elsie and her husband, Burt, were still a flight lower. Yes, she could safely say it. And it was her own prescription; she would say so. She'd had these pills almost a year. She didn't share Tobias' habit of taking chloral. No, these were a barbiturate, not so depressing.

But, in quantity, dangerous.

No, she would not attempt to say she'd given him the envelope. She would describe how she had shaken a few out into his hand and he'd said, "More," until she'd given them all.

The envelope was in her pocket. She would remember to crumple it up and throw it into the wastebasket in her room. His fingerprints would not be on the envelope, naturally.

Everything must be as natural as possible, under the circumstances.

Elsie must be the one to take the thermos jug down to his room. She herself would not enter that room until morning. Because, naturally, she never did enter it. (Not with Belle hanging there on his wall, she thought parenthetically.)

Now, why would she be going there in the morning? Ah, she'd remember, when they asked this question, how Thone had looked at her oddly, as he took the pills, and asked her, so oddly, to wake him early. She would pretend to see, too late, what was in his mind. That he had wanted her, his stepmother, to be the one. Not to shock his father . . . not to shock poor Elsie, who adored him . . . She, Ione, least close to him . . .

So she would go to his room, early, obligingly, and find him. But first, she would take the thermos jug into his bathroom and wash it out and . . .

Detail.

It was important to keep the necessary impression clearly in mind or one might overlook details.

She tasted the chocolate again, measured the quantity with her eyes, and nodded. "It's hot enough, I think, Elsie," she said fussily. "It mustn't boil. Will you put about—oh, two cups—into the thermos, please?"

Ione herself turned off the flame, went to look into the

icebox. Her voice went on smoothly about leftovers and to-morrow's problems. Elsie silently measured two cups into the thermos jug.

A little prick of impatience pierced Ione. What were they talking about, in there, in the studio? If Thone was telling them his plans—if, for instance, he were engaged, or looking forward too much—then it wouldn't wash.

Ah, no, she thought bitterly. They'll be in the past, yet, with Belle.

Sometimes, as now, if didn't seem that Belle was really dead.

She thought, and the thought was bitter and very clear, Belle still lives if the child of her body lives in the world anywhere! Child of Belle's body, and Tobias' body! Which was mine! thought Ione. She felt herself swell with the old familiar feeling. She, Ione, endured beyond anything. She was founded on a rock and the rock was her own will, and nothing, nobody, could move her. What was hers was forever hers. Forever and ever. Amen. Yes, amen. Time could not wear *her* brand away. She was not like other people. Belle would see! For ah, when the child was gone, then Belle was finished and wiped away and gone from the world at last!

"Elsie," she said quietly, "these vegetables from Thursday. Can't we clear them out?"

"If you're not going to use 'em." Elsie took up the sack of re-fuse, as Ione knew she would, and dumped old vegetables with it, carried it off. Oh, she knew Elsie, knew her grooves and how she ran in them.

Ione lifted the cork of the thermos and dropped in the pills with dainty care. She put the stopper back and dusted her palm.

She could hear Elsie slamming can covers out where the refuse went.

If she were quick . . . ! She snatched an empty cream bottle and poured into it a little of the chocolate left in the pan. She moved to the door to the hall and bent over and stood the bottle on the floor in shadow behind a screen. When Elsie came in, Ione had a cup to her lips.

"Very good, Elsie," she said primly, and set it down. Now Elsie wouldn't notice that any chocolate had gone. She would think Ione had tasted it from this quickly soiled cup. There was only the bare fleeting unimportant chance that she'd notice a vanished cream bottle. But it couldn't seem significant.

In the morning, after she'd used it, she'd wash the cream bottle, too, and put it back in some obscure kitchen corner. Detail. The thermos jug must be found innocently stained with undrugged chocolate. And so it would be found. It would be arranged. Quite so.

"Will you put the thermos in Mr. Thone's room, Elsie, please, and take a clean cup down?"

"Yes, ma'am."

Ione, the little chatelaine, moved off into the hall. Elsie's back could not see her stoop to pick up the bottle. She went down to her own room. It was safe to go down, since the thermos jug was still in the kitchen. The cream bottle would be safest and handiest down there on a shelf in her closet. If the chocolate it held were cold or even soured, it wouldn't matter. The stopper must be found out of Thone's thermos jug. Detail.

She threw the envelope into her basket, remembered to do that. She put on a little powder. She felt the good solidity, the pleasing sensation of being in control of her world. As was necessary. Ah, yes, one kept one's own counsel. One managed. And here on the spinning planet burned one spot of power. . . . She closed her fingers on her palm. Spin . . . spin . . . but I keep . . . In spite of everything. Yes, in spite of Belle.

When she came into the long studio that lay off to the east along the canyon rim, upstairs, she knew they'd been at it. Talking about her. Because they were silent.

She said, picking up her knitting basket, smiling, "Elsie made you some chocolate, Thone, for later."

"Why, thanks, Ione."

What if he weren't so avid for milk and chocolate as he had been that first visit after the Army? What if he didn't take any? She put on her glasses. Gold-rimmed, they rode her small nose. Her jolly little face was placid. Ah, well, then, another time. . . . Lamplight fell on her rosy, busy little hands.

Amanda, driving in the spring dark along Linda Vista, with the Arroyo falling off at her right, felt the lingering sick taste of her departure from home. Didn't like it. Didn't like it at all.

Still, one couldn't say, even to so generally swell a mother as Kate, "Mother, I've laid eyes on a man and I don't know why, but I must investigate. I'm attracted, damn it. And I am off, deviously, in a thoroughly snide and female manner, to wangle his acquaintance. To give myself a chance . . . because I've got to know what this amounts to."

So she'd said it was her art. She'd said this artist was important. She'd held out bait. Maybe if she talked to him about her ambitions, he would discourage her, and Kate would like that.

She'd said it was a wonderful introduction and she meant to use it. She'd said she didn't think it was in bad taste. She'd said he was probably interested in young artists anyhow. He ought to be. He'd looked very nice and kind, she'd said. And really, it wouldn't take long, from North Hollywood to the hills back of Pasadena. She'd be back early. Tell Gene to wait. "Oh, Mother, don't be stuffy!"

But Kate hadn't been stuffy. And it hurt. And Amanda didn't like it.

But when she thought of where she was going, she was almost unbearably excited. It had been easy to find out where to go. She'd telephoned the galleries and they'd told her.

She rehearsed again her little speech. It wasn't a speech to be said over the telephone, nor could she make an appointment to say it. No, she must just go, just barge in. . . .

Take her courage in her hand. Courage? Crust, thought Amanda. Oh, well, blame it on Art. She wanted to paint, ergo, she was a little bit crazy.

The car buzzed on. She looked to her left for the ascending road, found it, and was glad to have to concentrate on coaxing the car up and around the sudden mountain.

She parked as close to the wall as she could. Her palms held a dampness that wouldn't rub off. She crossed the shallow courtyard, stabbed at the bell. There. Now it was too late to hesitate.

4.

"Mr. Garrison?"

The old woman who opened the door had a dour and unresponsive face. "I'll see. What is the name?"

"Amanda Garth."

"Will you wait, please?" It was perfectly mechanical. The woman, a housekeeper, Mandy guessed, went off to the right, stepped down one step through a wide opening.

Amanda looked around the almost square hall in which she stood. At the very center, steps went down. The hole in the floor through which they descended was round and railed with wrought iron. To her left a screen half hid a room that she guessed to be the kitchen, since it had a linoleum floor covering. There were other doors, all closed. Off to the right was lamplight and the murmur of voices.

Amanda stood still. Then up through the flat archway swung the young man, Thone, and behind him the old servant crossed the hall to the kitchen.

"I am Mr. Garrison's son. Can you tell me what it's about?" He was cool and polite.

"No. I'm afraid I can't," said Amanda, as cool as he. "If Mr. Garrison is busy will you ask him when I *may* see him?"

He looked down at her with a faint smile, a remote, impersonal, patient smile. Then with a little shrug he turned and was gone through the arch. She could hear what he said, in there. It seemed to her that he meant her to hear. His voice was not loud but it had a carrying ring to it, as if he sent it back to her deliberately.

"It's the short-haired girl who was watching us down at the galleries today," Thone told his father. "Probably an art student. Do you want to bother, Dad?"

She didn't get the murmured reply. She fought off emotions that swarmed like bees. Anger, embarrassment, a little surprise that she had been noticed at all. The short-haired girl? Ah, so?

He came back, beckoning with a slow sweep of his arm. She walked past him with her chin up and he caught her arm quickly. "Whoops, the step!"

"Thank you," said Amanda. The place where he touched her was too vivid a mark. Amanda cut off her arm with a quick slash of inattention, and looked about her.

This big room was the artist's workroom. But around a fireplace there was a nookish arrangement of sofas and chairs. These were modern pieces with a built-in look. Mrs. Garrison, still in her gray, was knitting on something blue. She was at home in a corner of the sofa, cozy and passive. She wouldn't help. Her eyes, over her spectacles, were merely calm.

Tobias Garrison, one thin thigh over the other, dangled a foot to the fire. He did not rise. His sad eyes wavered nervously across his caller's face. "Yes?"

Thone, behind her, was silent. Amanda opened her lips and nothing happened. It was perfectly awful!

"Speak your lines, child," said Fanny Austin briskly. Next to Tobias, her ugly little face was bright and interested and not unkind.

Amanda felt the paralysis leaving her. She smiled at Fanny, threw "Thank you" with an eyebrow. She said, "I *am* an art student, Mr. Garrison. And I haven't quite as much n-nerve as I thought I had. I came because we've met before."

"Is that so?" Tobias' voice was smoother than she would have expected it to be. "I'm sorry. I don't remember you. Perhaps you'll remind me?"

Something touched the backs of her legs. Thone had brought her an armless chair. Amanda sat down with quite successful steadiness. She kept her back straight and leaned forward- "It was a long time ago, sir."

His head cocked politely.

She said, "Isn't it true, Mr. Garrison, that when your son was born, they showed you the wrong child?"

He straightened, where he sat, with shock. "That's so," he said. His eyes held hers now and she was aware of nothing else.

"I am the wrong child," said Mandy. "So you see, we have met, although I don't remember you, either."

"Well, mercy on us!" crowed Fanny, at last. "Please tell us more." Some tension of shock collapsed with her frank display of curiosity.

"Hence all that interest this afternoon," said Thone lightly. He moved in, near Fanny, and sat at the other side of a small round-topped table.

Amanda didn't look at him. "Of course I was interested," she admitted readily. "I only heard about it this morning. I went right down and stared as hard as I could."

Tobias gave her a rather shaky smile.

"Because you think perhaps we were swapped in the cradle?" Thone's voice was still light. Whether he was angry or amused, she couldn't tell.

"Did you know about it?" Amanda turned and looked straight at him.

"Oh, yes."

"Know *what?*" said Ione. Her hands had let the knitting fall. It lay tangled. "I don't understand. . . ."

"Oh, Mrs. Garrison," said Mandy, with a swift turn toward her, "I don't mean to come in here and pretend to think you're my mother. I don't think that at all. I—"

"I am no one's mother," said Ione shortly. Her eyes were very dark and had a rather blind and hostile look.

"Wait, wait," cried Fanny. "Tobias, tell us!"

"It was nothing," said Tobias. "But we have met before, true enough."

"That's right," said Amanda. "That's all."

Tobias smiled. "I must say I wouldn't have known you, my dear. I saw you this afternoon, of course. You made a nice bit of color." He was very kind. "But I do remember. It was a stupid mistake at the hospital, Fanny. I thought for a little while that I had a daughter. I take it this is she, grown up."

"You had a son," said Ione with some intensity.

"Of course, my dear."

"But how . . . ?" Her small hands looped the yarn furiously.

"It's nothing to be upset about," said Thone lazily. His head lay back on the chair. He was looking down his handsome nose. His forefinger played with the tabletop. It was on a swivel, somehow. It moved as he touched it.

Amanda was furious. "Of course it's nothing to be upset about. I . . . My father and mother are very . . . dear to me. I'm sorry I came. I thought," she spoke to Tobias, "if you remembered, perhaps you'd tell me some things I need to know about my work."

"For auld lang syne," said Fanny, nodding.

Amanda's anger died. "Oh, I am sorry," she said, in distress. "I never thought you'd think I thought . . . Yes, for auld lang syne, of course. That's all I meant."

"How is your father, my dear?" asked Tobias blandly. "He struck me as a very fine man indeed. John Garth. That's right?"

"He . . . isn't living. Not for twelve years."

"Ah, too bad. I never met your mother."

"Mother's fine," said Amanda. An expression of bewilderment possessed her face. "Was it your first wife, then?" she blurted.

"*I* am Mr. Garrison's first wife," said Ione, with odd finality.

And the silence rang.

"Oh, mercy on us, Ione!" cried Fanny. "Don't let the poor child imagine . . ." She bent to Mandy. "This Mrs. Garrison is both the first and the third, my dear. *Your* mother—I mean the wife who might have been your mother—was Belle. Belle Thone."

"'Belle in the Doorway'?" Amanda gasped. "Oh, I can't tell you . . . how that painting . . . struck me. It almost made me cry!" She was giving herself away, somehow. But she couldn't help it. It seemed important to tell the artist.

There was another awful silence.

"Belle herself never cared for that picture," said Thone, rather dryly and steadily, "did she, Dad?" Perhaps he was inviting his father to ride out emotion with chatter. Tobias didn't answer. His eyes were sunken. His face was drawn.

Amanda looked desperately about her. "Yes. She's dead," snapped Fanny. And Thone stirred in his chair. For a moment, wildly, Mandy saw herself being picked up and thrown out of this house. She started to get up. She was frightened.

But Ione said, pleasantly. "Perhaps you'd be interested in another portrait of Belle, Miss . . . Garth, is it? Would you mind, Thone, if I took her down to see it?"

"No, no," said Thone with a sharp movement of his hand. His eyes were on his father. "Show her. Go ahead. Take her down."

Take her away, thought Amanda. She followed the plump little lady up the step, then to the descending stairs that went down the middle of the house. Followed numbly, grateful to escape from something she'd caused and regretted and didn't understand.

Fanny thought it was rather decent of Ione to get the girl out of the room for a minute. "Toby, darling," she said aloud, "I'm sorry. Somebody had to tell her."

"Dad, if she's going to make you feel bad, let me ease her out. You needn't see her again, you know."

Tobias roused himself. "I'm all right. All right now. She . . . thrust me back." He crossed his legs the other way and let his head rest. "Seems a nice girl. Lovely face." Thone grunted. "You must remember," said Tobias gently, "that I was a pretty excited father that morning after you were born. You must try to understand this. I'm afraid I was full of high and exalted thoughts and feelings. I'm afraid I looked very hard and very long and greedily at the wrong little face. It robbed you of nothing. Never feel that it did. Yet . . . don't you see? That girl . . . We have met before."

"Of course I see," said Thone, just as gently.

The stairs went on down, but Ione led Mandy away from them at the first level they came to. She hadn't said a word. But at last, as she threw open a door at the end of the rectangular carpeted passage, she spoke. "This is Thone's room."

Mandy's heart thudded heavily. Ione reached within and found the switch. Lamps bloomed. Then Ione said, more a statement than a question, watching the girl's face in the new light, "You believe, perhaps, there was a real error in that hospital?"

I can be honest, thought Mandy stubbornly, although I've sure made a fool of myself. "Not really," she said, "but I did . . . play a little bit with the idea. Possibly I'm romantic or something." Her nervous smile asked for understanding and forgiveness.

"Your own mother told you about this?" said Ione coolly.

"Yes."

"Does *she* suppose . . . ?"

"Oh, no, no. We didn't even discuss it," said Mandy fiercely. "Because—well, we just know it makes no difference, anyway."

Ione's plump little face was closed, somehow. Calm, not angry, perhaps thoughtful. She said no more. She ushered Mandy into the room with a gesture.

The picture was hanging above a small corner mantel. Mandy didn't want to look at it, particularly. But she did. She drew nearer. It was a head and shoulders. It was Belle, and she was lovely.

But there wasn't the enchantment, Mandy thought, the elusive challenging life. The impression of radiance at which one must snatch, quickly, because it was as slippery as time. It would pierce your heart and go. This was Belle, lovely and beloved, but not so much caught as held. . . .

Mandy's thoughts strayed. Thone's room. As she stood with her back to most of it, her eye sought the wide window glass across which the curtains had not been drawn. It made a mirror against the dark. She could see the bookcases, half empty, the small desk, bare. The single bed, the night table. The dark tile floor whose insane coldness was covered, in part, by a thick fur rug. An uninhabited room. His suitcases . . .

Then she saw, in the glass, Ione lift her hand and strike out at something that stood on the night table. It fell with a crash to the hard floor. She leaped at the noise, turned.

"Oh, dear!" wailed Ione. "Oh, dear, look what I've done! My elbow! How stupid of me!"

But, thought Amanda, in dumb surprise, it wasn't your elbow. You did it on purpose. I saw you!

She went over to help, instinctively. She knelt, fumbling for an old handkerchief in her pocket somewhere. The stopper had come out of the dainty little thermos jug and liquid seeped forth.

Ione picked it up, as Amanda, head bent, dabbed at the floor.

"I dare say the insides are all in bits," said Ione worriedly. "He mustn't drink it, of course. Glass, you know. So dangerous. Oh, isn't that a pity!" She went trotting to an inner door, a bathroom. Water ran. "Yes, indeed. I'm afraid it is broken," she called back, rather cheerfully. "Don't touch that mess, my dear."

"I don't think it's hurt anything." Amanda looked at her handkerchief. A loathsome old rag, it had already been used to clean up a little oil paint once or twice. Now it was freshly stained with brown. She rolled the dampness inward and put it in her pocket. Her fingers found a clean one there, and she dried her hand on that.

Ione came back with a towel. "Thone's so fond of hot chocolate," she puffed, mopping. "Oh, well, it can't be helped. There. That will do, I think." Then suddenly, "Please let me have your handkerchief."

"Oh, no," said Mandy.

"Please," said Ione. Her hand, held forth, was steady and demanding. "You've soiled it. I will have it washed for you."

"Oh, please. Don't bother. It doesn't matter."

"But I insist." The jolly little face was smiling. The hand was still held out. It would never move, never retreat.

"It's just an old rag," said Mandy honestly. "You mustn't trouble."

"Not at all, my dear," said Ione, rather coldly. "I'll just take it, please. You shall have it again, once it is fresh." It was as if Amanda thought she'd steal it!

Amanda's face flushed. She thought, with a flare of antagonism, All right, you little fuss-buzz. "Very well," she murmured. But she didn't fish out the old rag. She put the cleaner bit of cloth—one of her best, she thought with satisfaction, and monogrammed, too—into that insistent hand. "Although it's hardly even damp, you see," she said.

"There now," said Ione, looking about with a sigh. "Have you looked enough?" She herself had not once glanced at the portrait.

"Oh, yes, quite enough, thank you. I'll go now," said Mandy. "I'm sorry if I—upset anything."

Ione laughed merrily. "It would seem that I've done the upsetting, now wouldn't it?" she said, twinkling. "I must tell poor Thone. Ah, well . . . Come along."

From the hall they could hear Fanny saying, "Only a week, Thone? Oh, too bad. But you must come and see me. Promise?"

"I'll be there," he promised. "Ah, Miss Garth." He got up.

Amanda took the one step down. She went to the older man. This time he rose. "I'm going now," she said. "Thank you, sir. Good night."

"Don't go." Whatever destroying emotion he had felt, it was gone. "Are you living out here, my dear?"

"Yes, in North Hollywood."

"Your people were living in the East at that time?"

"Yes, but Mother found a position out here. Mr. Callahan, of Callahan's Sons, is a friend."

"And you are studying?"

"Yes, sir, although I have a kind of part-time job, besides."

"You must come in the daylight," said he. "You must show me what you have been doing." Amanda gasped. "We must talk a little about painting. We are old friends," said Tobias.

Her puzzled heart melted. "I'd love to come again, if you're sure . . ."

"How about an afternoon?"

"May I? May I call you?"

"Please."

She gulped and swallowed. "I must get back. Good night, sir. Thank you." His hand was warm. "Good night, Miss Austin."

"Come and see *me*," invited Fanny. "I am a lonely old woman." This was a lie. "I'm at the Allwyn. I do love company." Fanny could say what she wished to say with that face of hers. It said to Mandy, "Child, *I'll* answer questions."

"You're very kind," said Mandy, blurting it. Oh, she did like Fanny Austin, the dear, charming old monkey-faced darling.

"Have you a car?" asked Thone politely.

"Yes, I have."

"Good night, my dear," said Ione.

"Good night, Mrs. Garrison."

"We shall see you again?" She was Mrs. Santa Claus, after all, so cute and jolly. The whole mysterious tension seemed to have vanished. Everyone was being nice.

Amanda said she hoped so, as Ione's hand touched hers a moment. Amanda walked, then, back to the hall, and Thone's hand came up to remind her of the step. She veered away from it, stepped up. They went out into cool darkness. She found the door handle of the car.

"Good night, Mr. Garrison."

There they were, out in the evening air, standing together in the road. He was much taller than she. His shoulder was level with her head. Mandy stiffened her neck, got into the car. He hadn't said good night. She put her key in the lock.

"Only one thing," said young Mr. Garrison quietly, and her foot trembled away from the starter. "You mustn't worry my father."

"Oh . . ."

"Only a few of us know how to speak to him of Belle."

"I *won't*," said Mandy.

Something about him softened. "Just talk about painting," he suggested lightly.

Her voice trembled. "That's what I came to do."

He stood there and said nothing. Mandy's face burned in the dark. Her toe pushed the button. The car's racket filled that humiliating silence. She said, as the motor quieted, sounding as light and gay as she could, "I may not see you again, Mr. Garrison. It's very nice to have met you. Good-by."

He stepped back, lifted his hand.

She backed down the mountain to the turn-around place with ferocious skill.

5.

The lunchroom swarmed with customers. Smell of coffee rose, dish-clatter of the post-movie rush hour. Drowsy husbands and dreamy-eyed wives ate silently, looking back on the show. Fellows and their girls, the show forgotten, stepped into roles in their own small dramas.

Mandy picked at the paper doily.

Gene Noyes pushed his cup away. "Late," he said. "Listen, Mandy, I'm going to take you home and dump you. You aren't here, anyway. You've got your mind on something else and I can't snap you out of it."

"That's so," she admitted. "I'm sorry."

"Let me in on it?"

She looked at his friendly face, his puzzled brown eyes, waiting for her to let him in. "Gene," she said, "see if you can make any sense out of this. If a woman deliberately . . ."

"Yeah. Go ahead."

Her fingernail took the scallops off the doily.

"Where were you tonight?" She looked up, startled. "Listen, Mandy, you know I'm kinda crazy about your mother. Whatever you were up to, it didn't set so well with her. I'd think about that, if I were you."

"Oh." She put her hands to her temples. "I know. You don't need to tell me."

"O.K.," he said. "I'm not scolding. I thought maybe you didn't know, that's all."

She smiled at him. "Gene, tell me this. Suppose you saw a woman deliberately knock a jug of hot chocolate over onto a hard floor, so that it broke, and the chocolate had to be thrown away. What would you think?"

"Who was supposed to drink the stuff? Was she?"

"Not she. Somebody else."

"I'd think she didn't want the other guy to drink it."

"But why not?"

"Maybe," he shrugged, "it wouldn't be good for him. Maybe he's too fat already."

"No."

"Well, then, maybe she's just mad at him. Wants to spoil his fun."

"Childish . . . ?"

"Yeah."

"No," said Mandy.

"O.K. Then maybe the stuff is poisoned."

"Don't be silly," said Mandy.

"Then he's a drug addict and takes his dope that way and she's trying to cure him."

"Oh, for heaven's sake!"

"Well?" He raised his brows at her. "What else is there?

You saw something like that, Mandy? That's what's eating you?"

"I can't understand it."

"Who fixed the chocolate for him?"

"I don't know."

"If it was just plain chocolate, that's one thing," said Gene cheerfully. "And if not, then it's something else again, hm?"

"Yes," she said, "of course."

"You'd have to start by finding that out. But if the stuff's gone down the drain, you're never going to find out. So why not skip it, Mandy?"

Mandy said slowly, "It's not quite all gone." He looked at the handkerchief she pulled out of her pocket, the stain that was revealed as she unrolled it.

"Magic of science, hm? And I'm a magician, too. I'm a chemist, you just remembered."

"Could you, Gene?"

"Um . . . maybe."

"Would you?"

He picked up the rag, looked at the stain, sniffed it. "What'll you give me?" he grinned.

"Oh, Gene, please!"

"You're pretty serious, Mandy."

"It was so strange," she said.

"You really want to know?"

"Yes."

"O.K.," he said. He put the handkerchief in his pocket.

"When, Gene?"

"In a hurry?"

"Well, I . . ."

"Frank Mitchell's got a pretty nice little lab he lets me fool around."

"Can't you do it at Callahan's tomorrow?"

"No."

"When, Gene?"

"You *want* this, Mandy? O.K. Early in the morning."

"I thank you," said Amanda.

"So I'll be up at the crack of dawn, and I don't even know what I'm doing. That's love, baby."

"Nuh-uh. Science!" said Mandy, dimpling. The rest of his date was livelier, Gene felt.

But as Amanda took off the yellow suit at last in her own room, restored to her from Cousin Edna's tenancy, she kept gnawing at that inexplicable incident. Thone's room, Thone's hot chocolate, for Thone to drink. If there had been anything wrong with it, then someone in that house was trying to harm him. Or, even if it was perfectly good plain chocolate, why did his stepmother think that he mustn't drink it? Did she *think* someone in the house wanted to harm him? Who? Why?

There could be someone living there whom Amanda hadn't seen. Maybe he even had a wife. Maybe that's why he was so—so distant. She thought of those suitcases, that male room. No, if he had a wife she wasn't with him. At least . . .

It's none of my business, Amanda told herself. I'll keep away. I won't go back there any more. I can make a fool of myself once and no harm done. If I forget about it now, stop it, drop it . . .

She scolded herself to sleep at last.

Between classes the next morning, she telephoned. "Gene?"

"Hiya, Mandy. How's it go?"

"Fine. Did you try to find out . . . what I wanted to know?"

"Oh, that. You know what was on that handkerchief, Mandy?"

"I'm asking you. You're the genius."

"By the way, I thought you were a lady. Call that a handkerchief?"

"I never said I was any lady." Mandy kept her voice patient and grimaced with the effort. "Come on, Gene."

"Hypnotic," he said. "One of those patented barbiturates, probably."

"But what *is* it?"

"Sleeping dope."

"Oh."

She heard him breathing in the interval. "Pretty stiff solution, Mandy," he said warily.

"What would it *do?*"

"Wouldn't do any good."

"Do you mean, like poison?"

"Yup. Quite a lot like poison. Fact, it is poison."

"Gene! Would it . . . is it enough to . . . ?"

"Hell, I dunno," he said irritably. "I'm no doctor. I'd say it was damn dangerous." His voice faded, came back stronger. "What are you going to do, Mandy?"

"I don't know," she whimpered.

"Maybe you oughta—"

"Where's the handkerchief, Gene?"

"I left it in the lab."

"Oh."

"Listen, Mandy, you keep away from whatever this is. Hear me? Why don't you tell somebody the whole thing? Tell me the story and *I'll* do something. Meet me for lunch, Mandy?"

"I—I don't know. I . . . ."

"At least you oughta tell the one who was meant to drink that stuff," he said sternly. "Give him a chance. Maybe it doesn't mean anything, but that way you'd be safer."

"You're *sure*, Gene?"

"Naturally."

"I'm sorry. I'll have to call you back."

"See me tonight? Mandy . . ."

"Maybe. Thanks. Good-by . . . so long. . . ."

Poisoned! And he might have . . . ! Oh, no! screamed Mandy soundlessly. No! She leaned on the wall of the booth. Students went by in the corridor, eleven-o'clock classes coming up, Easter vacation in the wind. They were walking in another world.

If it hadn't been for a date with Gene last night, the thought of poison might have grazed her mind and disappeared again. She would have gone on wondering, but never known. Not as she knew now. She wouldn't have this fact, like a boulder in the road. Couldn't go around it. There it lay.

So what was there to do? You go to the police, she thought. That's what you do. You tell them there was poison in a certain thermos jug in a certain house. They say, "How do you know?" You can show them how you know.

Then they say, "Who put it there?" You don't know.

"Why?" You don't know.

"Well, who got it?" Nobody got it. It was thrown away.

"Whatcha want us to do, lady?" Save him! Keep him!

"What's it to you, lady?" I don't know what it is to me, but he must not die!

Oh, no, that wasn't any good, not that way. No, the thing to do is go to him. Tell him. Warn Thone himself to be careful. That's much quicker, much better. That's direct. That is all the police would do, anyhow.

She found the Garrison number in the book. The housekeeper's voice said, "Hello."

"Mr. Thone Garrison, please." She didn't know how she was going to say this.

"He isn't in right now."

"Oh." She felt sick with disappointment. "When will he be back?"

"Not until late this afternoon. Can I give him a message?"

The wire sang. "No," said Mandy sadly, "no message."

She sagged against the wall. Then she pulled herself up and dialed the number again. "This is Amanda Garth," she said briskly. "I want to speak to Mr. Tobias Garrison, please."

"Mr. Garrison is busy just now." The same mechanical voice. "Can I give him a message?"

"Please just ask him if Amanda Garth may come to see him today." The line was empty for a minute or two and Mandy closed her eyes, walking in the square hall, stepping one step down.

"Mr. Garrison suggests tomorrow at two."

"Not today?" she wailed. Then quickly, "All right, yes. That will be fine. I'll be there tomorrow."

She hung up, gnawed her thumb. Tomorrow. She snatched at the book again. No, Fanny wasn't listed. But wait, she had been told . . . The Allwyn. She got it, asked for Miss Austin's apartment.

Fanny said, "Yes?. . . Oh, yes, my dear?"

"May I come to see you?"

"Of course. When would you like to come?"

"Are you busy now?"

"Now?" Wonder at this urgency sung over the wire. Then Fanny said, "Why don't you come and take lunch with me, Amanda? I have three or four important people here whom I will firmly get rid of."

"Oh, thank you," Amanda choked.

"You interest me," said Fanny. "You come along."

6.

Mandy was calmer by the time she got to Fanny's. Her hostess's shrewd eyes took in this fact at once. Mandy found herself welcomed with a blunt and most warming eagerness. Fanny was curious and she didn't care who knew it. Fanny said, "Sit down, you pretty thing, and ask me questions. I am intrigued. I did enjoy your entrance yesterday. I never heard of such a thing as this baby business. Belle never mentioned it to me. You did hit a snarl up there, now, didn't you?"

"Oh, I didn't mean . . ."

"*You* couldn't know how many wives there'd been or in what order, my dear. I realize. Nor did you look the fool you felt."

Mandy's eyes filled with tears.

"Now, there," said Fanny. "I thought I'd tell you. Tobias is pleased, I assure you. He feels a bond. You made him remember a very high point in his life. That's all that ailed him. My girl will stir us up a little food, right here. We can be comfortable."

Mandy mopped her eyes. She said, muffled in the handkerchief, "I think you're wonderful!"

"Well, say it loud!" crowed Fanny. "Of course I'm wonderful! And I'm getting old and I like to hear it. I shan't hear through the sod, you know, or smell my pretty flowers." She patted Mandy's knee. "Who buys your clothes?"

"I do." Mandy was wearing a rosy pink dress, cut simply from thin wool, trimmed with silver buttons, and over it a paler pink short belted fuzzy coat. Black kid round-toed, flat-heeled shoes on her feet and a black kid bag swung on her shoulder.

"You're very clever," said Fanny. She herself was in emerald green, like a parrot.

"I'm going to be a designer," Mandy told her. "Not clothes. Fabrics."

"Mmmm." Fanny's eyes dimmed. She was looking into the past. "Dearest Belle, when I first knew her, wore such dull things. Always beige or gray or black. Then, after she married Toby, how she blossomed! I remember her clothes. When I saw her last, in New York, there was an outfit of forest green with red-brown, perfect to the last detail. She wore it like a costume. Always the hat, the shoes, the scarf. She never varied it. She had a rosy ball gown, rose and gold, and a golden rose for her hair. And there was a slate-blue dress with a purple jacket, impossible! But just right. I can see her gloves. I asked her once. A woman in a shop did those things for her. Belle herself didn't care, but Toby liked it, so she wore what he liked. Always just so, the same necklace with the same gown, designed together." Her eyes came back. "You want to hear about Belle, don't you?"

"Oh, yes! About all of them."

"Tobias married Ione long, long ago, when they were both young. Her name was Philips. He had a little money, so he could afford to paint, and he worked very hard, I think. When at last he began to be known, they bought that canyon house. It was nearly alone on the mountain, then. I forget who built it. Some mad soul. And they lived along.

"I've known them since 1919. Tobias painted my picture. We liked each other heartily. I introduced him to Belle in 1922. Belle Thone."

"What did she do?" asked Mandy.

"Do? Belle? She toiled not, neither did she spin." Fanny swayed in the chair. "She didn't do. She was. I wish I could show you Belle. She was a rare creature. Something she was made it enough just to be with her. Beauty? Yes, she was lovely to see. Many a movie chap thought he'd put her on the screen and reap his millions. But she didn't photograph, they found. Actually, it wasn't her looks at all. It wasn't her mind, although she had a mind that ranged and wondered and responded, magically. You could say anything to Belle. Anything at all! And you knew that, immediately. I suppose," mused Fanny, "it was what we call spirit, because that's the only word there is and it's sufficiently vague.

"Anyhow, I loved her. Everybody was drawn to her. And she never seemed to try, or even to close her hand to hold you. It wasn't that she pulled. It was as if something pushed you from behind and you went helplessly toward Belle, though she herself was free. Free even from the responsibility of having pulled at you. I'm being very obscure, my dear. I like to try to say it. However, to descend a little, she was quite rich. She was an heiress and an orphan. Such an advantage!

"Oh, young men in droves wanted to marry her. But she was twenty-eight before she married.

"Tobias had a wife already and it wasn't that he didn't care for Ione. He did and he does. But Ione . . . isn't careable-about. . . .

Now, there's a phrase for you!" Fanny stopped and frowned. "Of course," she went on in a moment, "I worshiped Belle. So did Toby. He fell on his knees. The worst thing about it, Belle did the same thing. Something magically deep and close, I think, began to flow between them, instantly. It happened like lightning. He painted 'Belle in the Doorway'."

"I understand," said Mandy.

"Yes." Fanny conceded that she understood. "So that's the way it was. So he and Ione were divorced. There were no children. Oh, it was very, very tough for Ione, you know. I do admire the way she took it."

Mandy said, puzzled, "She just stepped out?"

Fanny looked thoughtful. "Now, Ione is a possessive woman," she said. "You'll notice that. What's hers is hers."

I have noticed, thought Mandy. She remembered the catalogue, the fountain pen.

"And that must have made it even harder," Fanny went on, "for her to do what she did. They let me know the trouble they were in, of course. I loved them all. So I was—in it. I was here on the coast that winter. Oh, she felt it bitterly, I know. And so did Toby. It nearly killed him. And so did Belle. Yet, of three anguished people, Ione seemed the least distressed. Perhaps she was stunned.

"There was only once I thought she'd split—I thought she'd burst with her hurt and her pain. It was one afternoon. But, do you know, she— Something happened that day. She clamped down, as if the iron entered her soul. I saw it . . . lock. I will always remember."

Fanny's face was changing. It was wild and anguished for a

moment and then it closed. The mimicry was exquisite. Amanda, in one vivid glimpse, saw Ione's face that day.

"So she let him go," said Fanny, "not without grace, either. The divorce went through. Ione had an accident about this time. An auto struck her in the street. Tobias poured out every cent he had; he gave her all of it. She lay in a hospital for months. Lay quietly. I saw her. I was so sorry. But Tobias and Belle, with Belle's money, I suppose, went East."

"That's why they were there when—in 1924—"

"Yes, when Thone was born. When you were born, my dear."

"Isn't Thone . . . like his mother?" asked Mandy painfully.

"Not in looks at all," said Fanny judiciously. "In charm? Whatever it was? Yes, maybe. But it's not Belle! Not her own! Oh, you don't know. You never saw her alive."

Fanny drew her little body out of the chair. "She would stand," said Fanny, and suddenly she was taller and all grace, "she would turn her foot . . ." The actress turned her foot and then her arm swung over until her right hand rested on the left side of her neck. She nestled her chin against it. "She would do this," said Fanny, "all dreamy-eyed, and everybody would wait, while Belle remembered. It's a corny gesture, isn't it?"

"No. No, I see!" said Mandy.

Fanny's eyes kindled. "And when she didn't follow what you were saying, when she didn't understand your thought, she'd drop her head and close her eyes and put her hands flat along her cheeks." Fanny was doing what she described. Finger tips at her temples. "And you'd wait. Then Belle would lift her face and drop her hands and open her smiling eyes and say, 'I see!' And you'd be delighted! Delighted!

"She would sit in a chair," said Fanny, sitting. "She was always lithe and young to the day she died. She would sit and clasp her hands around her knees with her ankles crossed, and her feet wouldn't touch the floor. Alert, back straight, balanced. You see?"

Fanny dropped the pose. "I think skirts were longer." She brooded a minute. "Sometimes she would laugh without a sound." The marvelous old face wreathed in a smile, the chin tipped slowly up, and the head went back. Belle's ghost, in Fanny's chair, laughed without sound.

"Oh, my bag of tricks," said Fanny, suddenly sullen, "won't bring her back."

"But you—you do," gasped Mandy. "Mr. Garrison must have painted her often."

"Oh, he did, and he didn't. Most of those things he did in the islands have been sold. He only cares for one, you see. 'Belle in the Doorway'."

"But she . . . Is it true that Belle didn't like it?" Mandy squeaked with surprise. "Thone said . . ."

"I think that is true. She liked the one Thone keeps. That's why he keeps it. Belle wasn't awfully keen on painting. She let it alone. It was her husband's business. I never heard her criticize or praise. He never asked her to, that I heard."

"Does—is Thone a painter?"

"No. No, he's not. No interest, as far as I know. He's studying with an architect. Thone has Belle's money, you see, my dear. Belle made no will." Fanny's lips writhed. "She had no time. But Toby kept it all in trust for him. Quite a lot of money it is, still."

Fanny's glance became both shrewd and kind. "Also, he is a

very attractive young man, especially to girls. He had a most unfortunate experience. I think perhaps if I tell you . . . Once, a year ago, some little fool he'd taken around jumped from her father's office window. It was a pretty dreadful thing."

"How terrible!" gasped Mandy.

"Yes, too bad. Too bad. It's made him unnaturally wary and suspicious. He knows, of course—he concedes that although she died, poor little soul, and the worms are eating her, it was not for love. But, you see, she wrote a letter to his father. She left a note. Poor miserable, confused little fool!" Fanny exploded. "I suppose it was a blind revenge. Somebody else was going to have to feel bad . . . made no difference who. Oh, people, people! I do despair!" Fanny clasped her hands.

"Poor Thone. It changed him. Now he doesn't dare be as friendly and gay as he might want to be with his own generation. He didn't care for that girl, but she wrapped up all her woes and put them on his head. So he can't help wondering if, as he took her around, just playfully, just for fun, he somehow allowed her to expect too much. It's what she wrote. The little idiot! It hurt him and it frightened him. He can't entirely absolve himself. And, besides, quite naturally, he does wonder what goes on inside the mysterious heads of silly young girls."

"He isn't m-married?" stammered Mandy.

"Heavens, no. Furthermore, I should venture to say," said Fanny boldly, "he'll do no experimenting with friendship for a while yet. There'll be nothing tentative, no feelers out for love. He'll take no chances, Amanda. No girl will know if Thone cares for her company until, suddenly, when he's certain, there he'll be."

Mandy felt the color in her face. She said simply, "I'm glad you told me. I was all ready to experiment with friendship. He is very attractive."

"Of course he is. Of course you were. Naturally," said Fanny, beaming and nodding. "Ah, our lunch is coming in."

Mandy woke out of the spell the old lady had woven and remembered suddenly why she'd come. They sat at a little round table and Fanny served a salad daintily.

Amanda said uneasily, "Everybody likes Thone?"

"Oh, yes, indeed," said Fanny, twinkling at her. "Elsie and Burt idolize him. His father worships him. I'm head over heels in love with the boy myself. I don't know how they felt about him in the Army, of course." She made a face, laughing.

"Who are Elsie and Burt?"

"The couple up there. The servants."

"You've left out Ione."

"So I have," said Fanny, frowning a little. "But of course, she likes him. After all, she hardly knows him. You see, Belle died, and Thone and Tobias were heartsick. They had to plunge into some kind of life, and not the same kind, either. One young, only seventeen. The other getting old. Well, Ione rallied around and Toby needed her badly, badly. . . ."

"I'm sure Thone saw the lay of the land. He was at school. He nipped off and wiggled into the service. He's been away from home nearly all the time since they've remarried."

"When did Belle die?"

"She died out here, after they came back. They went off to the islands and foreign parts when Thone was four. It was rumors of war that brought them back again. Let's see. In 1941 they were in New York and so was I. In 1941, that fall, before our war, they came back to the canyon house. Thone was seventeen. Tobias was fifty-nine. Belle was forty-seven when she died."

"In the canyon house!" gasped Mandy.

"Oh, yes, my dear. When I think," said Fanny, "of Belle's death in that particularly stupid accident, I am like whoever it was who put it in a poem. I am not reconciled. At least I wasn't," she went on. "I was enraged with Providence for years. Now . . . well, we can remember her alive. She rests and we remember. And all goes well enough without her." The actress brooded.

Amanda said, "Accident?"

Fanny whipped herself to attention. "And I shan't enjoy telling you this part," she snapped, "but I intend to tell you all of it. Tobias has a stupid habit. He gets himself wound up periodically. Mind and imagination will not stop. He cannot sleep. He gets more tired and more tense. It spins up like a spiral. So he takes to chloral hydrate. After his dinner, every evening, a moderate dose. Nothing in the least dangerous. His heart is strong. He goes to bed early, then, and in a week or so he has broken up the tension and then he we ns himself from the drug.

"Well, one night somebody telephoned the house with news of a lost picture. Tobias wanted it back most desperately. Whoever called had it, would give it up. I don't know. . . . Anyhow, it so happened that only Belle was fit to go on this errand. Tobias had a mean cold. Elsie and Burt were off. It was a Thursday. Thone, poor kid, had a busted bone in his foot and was in a cast.

"So Belle would go. She was never afraid. Nobody thought she should be afraid.

"They called her a cab.

"Now, this is the maddening stupid thing. Belle never drove their car if she could help it. She didn't even have a driver's license. If she had gone in the cab, then the fact that somehow, some way—nobody knows—she'd got a dose of Toby's chloral wouldn't have mattered. She'd have passed out in the cab. But she wouldn't have died!

"No," said Fanny bitterly, "on this night, this wicked night, for some reason we can't even guess, Belle chose to drive herself. To change her mind, dismiss the cab, and go down alone, down the terraces in back to the garage, the only one they had then. The single garage at the bottom of the canyon on the lower road.

"So she opened the doors and started the car, and the tricky hooks on the doors weren't good. The doors blew closed. She must have got out, leaving the motor running, to jam the doors open again. But the chloral . . .

"She slumped down, she was on the floor, right under the exhaust. The doors stayed closed or blew again, who knows? They began to worry hours later. They didn't find her until almost morning."

"Oh . . ." moaned Mandy.

"He never got the stupid picture back, either," said Fanny viciously and clicked her teeth.

"Well," she went on in a minute, "I came as fast as I could. Ione was around."

"She . . . was?"

"Oh, yes. She'd been here all these years. I saw her now and again as I flitted through. She went into real estate and was a very successful businesswoman. You wouldn't think so, but she was. Still with that iron determination not to break. But when Belle was gone she came straight to Toby and he leaned on her. And she took care of everything."

And got him back, got her own back, thought Mandy. She said aloud, fearfully, "I suppose they were always . . . sure it was an accident?"

"Yes, yes." Fanny was not shocked. She herself had once taken this line of thought.

"But . . . Ione couldn't have . . . *liked* Belle."

"No," said Fanny. "Yet, it isn't *that* that keeps us from speaking of Belle before her. You must know this. Ione would listen calmly enough. But Toby knows what he did to *her*, you see, and there is his guilt, which makes him uncomfortable. Besides," she added impatiently, "though she might be willing, Ione can't talk about Belle. She never knew her. And hers is such a little tense and limited mind. It's small and full of details. If Toby stays within her bounds too much, why, that's the price he pays because he needs her."

"I don't understand her," Amanda said tremulously. "She—"

But Fanny looked stern. "My dear, Ione behaved admirably. And believe me, she had nothing to do with the accident to Belle. That's sure. She wasn't there. Not in the house, you see. Oh, she had called on them, I think. After they came home. Being very sporting. But, my dear, all those years! Oh, no, no. She's too little, Amanda, for so grand a passion. Besides, it wasn't possible."

Amanda stared into her tea. She thought, Who knew there was poison in the chocolate? Ione knew it! How did she know? Because she put it there. Not his father, not the servants, not Fanny, but Ione had a reason. Ione must have at least disliked Belle, and this was Belle's son. Oh, yes, it must be that she knew it was there because she'd put it there. She didn't want it found, not even on the handkerchief. It's plain she knew the poison was there. She didn't want it . . . used.

She must have changed her mind.

Why did she change her mind? A rocket burst in Mandy's head. On account of me! Because, suddenly, I appear! Maybe Thone isn't Belle's child! Maybe I am! She begins to wonder!

Mandy began to tremble.

"You haven't enjoyed hearing it, either," said Fanny grimly. "Come, come away from the table. My dear, are you going to see Tobias again?"

"Yes," gasped Mandy. "Tomorrow."

"They fascinate you." Fanny was kind. "But why do you feel afraid?"

"He might be my father. Belle might have been my mother," said Mandy whitely.

"Ah, no," said Fanny, still not unkindly. "You were very cute last night. It was very appealing. But you mustn't be fantastic. You mustn't be serious. And you mustn't meddle or cause confusion."

Somebody rang the doorbell. Fanny patted Amanda's shoulder and went to let in a man. Amanda never knew his name. Fanny had poured out all she had to say. For her, their private talk had reached an end. Amanda let it go.

She sat a minute more and rose to leave.

Belle was at rest. Fanny remembered her alive. Fanny was reconciled. Amanda wouldn't meddle with that.

She must, however, warn Thone, who was safe for a little while only, in the confusion.

o

It was a bad night. She tried to telephone again. She had missed him. Thone had been in and gone out again for the evening.

Gene telephoned in dismay. Frank Mitchell had ignored the note he'd left on a scrap of paper, come into his laboratory, and burned what to him looked like an old rag. Mandy said it didn't matter. She fended Gene off. She said she thought it was all right. She understood it, now. She hoped . . . she was pretty sure . . .

And then there was Kate, asking no questions. So Mandy tried to chatter and describe that place and how people had looked. She had, also, to excuse herself for playing hookey to see Miss Austin. The celebrated Miss Austin. It tasted bad in her mouth.

It hadn't gone well, either. She wasn't telling Kate enough and she knew Kate knew this. But Kate's first reaction, she also knew, would be to leap and stand between Mandy and any evil thing.

No one could stand between. She had to do this herself. Warn him. Tomorrow. Tomorrow was an eternity away.

She lay in bed and told herself doubts. Gene wasn't used to that kind of chemical test. Maybe he was mistaken. But then would come the memory of Ione demanding her handkerchief. Why? Because she knew. She knew, because the poison was there, and it was there, because she knew. . . . Mandy sat up and rubbed her head.

She went over and over all Fanny had told her. She found herself seeing Belle. From the portraits, and all the little mannerisms Fanny had shown her, how she looked, what she wore, her clothes . . .

No matter what Fanny thought, Thone was like his mother. Or why did she feel herself going, going toward him, helplessly, although he stood and made no sign and was himself quite free.

She lay back and a sick fear shook her. What if it should happen tonight? What if all she imagined and thought she could guess was wrong? Wrong! What if only the fact—poison in his room, waiting for him—what if that was all she ought to believe? She was only guessing who and why and why not! She didn't know. But poison in his room had waited once. It might wait again.

She writhed on the bed. Telephone? No, you can't telephone in the night. And who is to guarantee that evil itself wouldn't answer?

Mandy rolled. She began to repeat, "Now I lay me . . ."

As early as she dared, she telephoned to confirm her appointment. The housekeeper's voice was placid. No, nothing had happened during the night, or surely no such placid voice would answer. Mandy put her head on her arms, and Kate, coming through the room to breakfast, saw, hesitated, bit her lip, went on.

7.

Ione, snug and proper in her three-piece black, zipped expertly through traffic while the white lace fluttered on her hat. She drove with the top down. People nudged each other and said, "Oh, look! How cute! Look at that dear little old lady in the swanky car. Isn't she wonderful?" She drove very well. She loved expensive automobiles. Tobias had grown to like them, too. He'd had a Cadillac, the year Belle died. Such a quiet engine. Idling, one could scarcely tell it was running. . . .

Six years ago. And yet, this Tuesday morning, here she was, driving herself in this direction on this errand because of Belle's vivid presence in her house. There was nothing else to do. She couldn't question Toby too intensely. She'd go and see this woman and find out. And get rid of her own phrase that kept haunting her: Belle still lives if the child of her body . . .

A notion, she knew. It was Thone who invoked the woman's presence, because, blood or no blood, she lived in his memory. Yet, here came this girl to re-create Belle twice over in Toby's mind, to raise her from the dead all over again. What would be the use? she thought impatiently.

Well, she would see what it amounted to. She would then

know what had to be done. It had been many years ago that she had first seen what had to be done.

Belle, one terrible afternoon, with that maddening careless-ness, that odd surrender to Fate, had made it clear. Oh, yes; Belle, saying with that searing pity, "Ione, if it hurts too much, we needn't . . . I can do without. I can go away. I will go."

For just a moment it was clear that Ione could have held on, could have insisted, could have kept him. There need have been no divorce. "He can't bear this!" she'd said, that Belle.

Nor could he bear that! Ione had seen. She saw through Belle's eyes, queerly, how it was with Toby. And in that moment she had known that no matter whether she kept the shell or let it go, Toby was never to be hers again unless Belle was not in the world. Anywhere. Until Belle died!

So she had seen what had to be done. Belle herself had shown her. Seen it hard and clear and locked the knowledge away. Belle must die and Ione must live.

So one must plan a little.

And then, stupidly, so lost she'd been in that resolve, in that grim need, she'd walked heedlessly into the path of a car and been hurt, and had had to wait.

Wait a long, long time.

But she'd leaned on her fierce inner purpose. No one knew what propped her up. It was not necessary to confide in anyone. Not for her. She fed on her own thoughts. Proudly. Then and always. Never, never, no matter how long, would she have surren-dered the dark source of her strength in those days. She hadn't been idly dreaming. To dream it were done would have weakened the doing. She guarded against that. She dreamed how she would do it . . . only how. And at last they'd drifted back within her reach.

It hadn't been difficult.

She went to call. Waited to be announced. Gleaned what she could, there alone in the hall. The hall of the canyon house. It was hers, now. Not then. She had refused it because it was only half hers, in those early days. But she'd gone through it, all the same, after she had recovered and they were gone, in the East. She had taken a hard and icy satisfaction in combing out of it all those things that were hers alone. Every tiniest thing. Including the small foot-square painting Tobias was so fond of. He had called it hers one day, and she chose to consider it her property, taking his careless words literally, although she knew how much he cared for it. She had never confessed that seizure. He'd thought it lost or stolen.

It had been useful.

Odd, now, how she couldn't remember what she'd seen in the canyon house that day, or taken, except those things that later had been useful. She'd looked in the drawer and known where to find the extra set of keys for his car, and the spare garage key, too, there in the same spot, tucked far back, where they'd kept such things of old habit. She'd snatched up the blue scarf—Belle's, of course—stuffed in there, and hidden it in her bag. What else? There must have been something else. But these were all she had really needed.

Then she'd been summoned to the studio to meet a thinnish restless boy with his foot in a cast, to endure Tobias' inquiring looks, to note he was getting one of his heavy colds, to hear that he was back at his chloral. To endure Belle's quiet presence (sitting there with her arms around her knees like a schoolgirl!). To say to Elsie, as she went away with bits of a plan already whirling in her head, "Elsie, I wondered if you could clean for me, some Thursday." And Elsie had said, "We're off around one o'clock, ma'am, same as always."

So Thursday had come along.

The telephone call at the lonely outdoor booth near the gas station, only a short way from the mountain road. Her handkerchief over the mouthpiece, blurred voice, hinting of a conscience-stricken thief. She'd said she was in Long Beach. She'd meet them halfway. Named a drugstore, one of a bright busy chain. Belle mustn't be afraid to come. Hinted that they were leaving the state, this muffled-voiced female and her mythical thieving husband. Hinting that the impulse to return the picture would last only a little while.

Thone couldn't come. Burt wasn't there. Belle wouldn't let Toby do it, with his cold and his chloral. She'd take a cab, naturally. Ione knew, because she'd watched. Belle rarely drove the car and then not far.

So . . . quick . . . up the mountain and her own car hidden at the turn-around place, facing down. She'd crossed the road and stood in the shadow of the deodar tree. All of it was so tentative. Until the very last, the way was open to go back.

If Belle came out of the house before the cab, why, another time . . .

But the cab came first.

She'd pulled Belle's blue scarf over her hair and around her face and stepped out of the shadow and called to him. She'd given him money. Said she'd changed her mind. She'd told him to go on up and around the canyon. He could get down the other side.

Then stuffed the scarf away, quickly, and when Belle came out, they'd met at the gate.

"I wanted to talk to you. Are you going out?"

"My cab . . ."

"I just saw a cab. I wonder if he's lost. He went on up the road. Let me drive you."

"Too far," she'd said.

"Then just down the mountain to a cab stand. Please. I do want to talk to you . . . about Toby. I'm worried. Isn't he well?"

Belle had pity. That was her weak spot.

"*I* have no child," Ione had said. So Belle had gone with her to the car. Still, the way back was open.

She'd pulled up under the tree in the darkest spot at the drive-in stand. Thirsty. Belle must have something too. In a hurry? Oh, then Ione would fetch them something quickly. She'd left the car and fetched them soft drinks. Asked for a double dose of sirup, she remembered. Easy to put the chloral in one of them. She'd had it ready, of course.

It would have been simpler, in a way, to give her too much chloral and let it go at that. But she had thought it all out. If one gave Belle a lethal dose and put her in a cab, how could one be sure that the cabby wouldn't get her to a hospital . . . too soon? And Belle, saved, could say too much. So, if one had to take her to a lonely spot anyhow, why imperil the impression of an accidental drugging? One paper of the stuff by accident, yes. But hardly several. So she'd used just Toby's normal portion.

And then, she remembered, made a little emotional scene so

that Belle, eager to escape, would down even this bitter drink quickly, to get it over.

Then, stalling, pretending to be on the way to a cab stand, a little driving, until she slept.

And still, she wasn't dying. Oh, yes, better this way, much better. A way back could have been found, even yet, had there been anything wrong. If, for instance, there had been any lovers parked in the lower canyon road

But there hadn't been anyone there.

So, to creep, without light, up the bottom of the canyon, to take Belle's shoes and slip them on her own feet, her little feet. To unlock the doors of the garage (a padlock, not a bar inside, as now). To walk in, remembering to make a pattern with her footprints, in case. Start the motor, the quiet expensive motor. Walk backward to the steps that came down from the garden, the lowest terrace. Take the steps themselves backward, two feet to a step on alternate steps and then down again, two feet on each skipped step. (Belle would have come down so gingerly.) Then out to the street where the car, pulled close, was not even visible from the big house hanging above.

Then the brink. The final leap over. After this, there was no way back.

To lift, with the strength one can find if one has to, with care lest she wake, oh, with soft strong care, Belle's body from the car. To leave it on the floor. Shoes returned to the proper feet. Blue scarf knotted around Belle's neck. Belle's flashlight from her purse on the floor near her hand. Doors left as if they'd fallen shut.

A moment to work at the hooks, to make them slippery and

insecure by a little bending. Her whiskbroom on the concrete apron, a handful of dust. The car started softly, steering wheel not turned. Who could say that it had *stopped?* A swing around the dead end of the canyon, back, out, away.

Home. Where her light had burned all evening in her sitting room, behind drawn blinds. Softly, softly, into the alley.

And to wait.

How full of strength and calm she'd been for Toby!

So many boys had been killed in the war!

But one can't just hope, she thought impatiently.

She began to peer about for the building she sought. Yes, there it was. Callahan's Sons, Fine Fabrics, Los Angeles.

8.

Tobias was at her service, Amanda found. He was alone in the long room. He was waiting for her. This hour was hers.

The house was very quiet and it had an empty ring to it. Light in the studio was abundant and calm and the northern glass showed, on this clear day, the mountains in a high band across the sky. There was peacefulness here that penetrated to her taut nerves, plucked at tight strings so that she could almost hear them twang.

She felt shaky. She put down her two canvases that she'd brought. Her hand was moist and she was ashamed of it. She thought he must read in her face the frightful hours of the night behind her.

Tobias himself was at ease and prepared to be very sweet to her. His deep-set eyes were steady with kindness. He had her sit down; he asked her questions about the school and the courses she was taking. She found herself describing Miss Alice Anderson and seeing that fervid soul with a new eye, the eye of his maturity, so that Miss Anderson's passion was put in a new proportion.

"Has she seen your pictures?" he asked.

"Yes, but she . . ." Mandy struggled, "she looks right over my head. I know I can't paint very well. I haven't had enough practice. But even so, isn't it possible to tell whether I have any right to try? I know," she went on boldly, "that most people can't help feeling they have something important in themselves. That what they see or feel has a deep and special meaning. And I know, sometimes, it isn't important at all, and the one who feels it is the last to realize . . . how commonplace it is."

He was smiling at her. "That's not a common remark, young lady. So far, so good. Now come . . . let me see."

She said, still hesitating, "I really want you to tell me."

"*I* may not be able to tell you," he warned. "There's a great deal outside my range, you know."

"You say what you think," said Mandy with a comical air of indulgence with which she laughed with him in a warm glow, as if they were queerly and exhilaratingly equals now, because each was humble in his own place.

She'd brought a little landscape, a spare thing, a limited vista, a piece of the garden wall, the texture of the walk, bark on the tree trunk. It was too difficult for her. Yet she felt it would show her desire.

He looked, silently.

The other one was a glimpse past Kate's cheek and the nape of her neck at still life on a table. Mandy felt for the hundredth time that it really wasn't very good, and yet there had been something she'd been after.

Tobias looked, silently.

Amanda was lost, cased in a trance of wondering, of not unpleasant suspense. She'd forgotten all about anxiety or evil, past or present. Her mind marched with the artist's, or at least limped behind. The tumultuous world of other people was far away.

Thone came upon them so. She heard him and looked up and her mood burst into fragments of emotion.

He advanced to a spot behind his father's shoulder. Tobias knew his step and his presence without turning. "What about these?" he asked.

Thone said, instantly, of the landscape, "That's good." And of the other, "That's bad."

Tobias smiled at Mandy's astonished face. "*His* opinion. Quite worthless," he said, half humorously. He let the still life fall and studied the other. "So muted?" he said. "I miss some color."

"But I saw it like that," insisted Mandy. "I wanted . . ." She didn't go on.

He murmured, "Yes."

"I like it very much," said Thone firmly.

"Yes." Tobias moved a brow. "You would. I see that you would."

"She's surrounded a piece of air. She painted a hunk of space. She coralled it."

Mandy, with saucer eyes, felt her heart go down on figurative knees.

"Ye-es," said Tobias. He took up the other. "In this there is a little more finesse."

"Not much," said Mandy cheerfully.

"It's gooey," pronounced Thone. "Sentimental." He grinned at her. "Not that you asked me."

"I'm not against sentiment," said Amanda stoutly, and she closed her lips on the rest of her thought.

Tobias shook his head. "The point is, my dear, if you want

to paint pictures, you will paint pictures. If you like the feel of doing it, if you get lost in it, then, good or bad, you'll paint them. What you want from me is the promise of a career? Of value to the world, shall we say?" She nodded. "Shall you go head over heels into this, and drop everything else?" He cocked his head.

Mandy got up and touched her pictures as if to lay them ready for departure. "I needn't have asked you or anyone," she said. "Because I know exactly what I'll do. I'll paint for fun. For my own best fun. And if anything comes of that, let it. But I wouldn't dare go head over heels, as you say. It's too presumptuous. I couldn't do it. Not," said Mandy with great firmness, "at my age."

Tobias dissolved into tender laughter. Thone stood with his hands in his pockets, smiling at his father's pleasure. And it was wonderful! Amanda felt herself to be, for once, perfectly happy.

Elsie poked her head in. "Mr. Peck is on the phone, sir."

And suddenly the older man had gone. She and Thone were alone together and the ripples of her happiness widened and lessened and faded into calm and then calm shattered with the upthrust of fear and the necessity and the opportunity for what she must do. Now! Now, she must tell him.

It was very difficult. It was almost impossible. She didn't know how to begin. She had to just blunder, slam bang, into the warning. There wouldn't be much time. In the background of her mind there persisted the thought that she mustn't worry his father. So she must hurry.

She said, "Mr. Garrison, someone tried to poison you Sunday night. There was poison in the chocolate in your room. Your stepmother knocked it over." She stopped for breath.

He said levelly, "What the devil are you talking about?"

"You see, I got some on my handkerchief. I had it analyzed."

"You *what?*"

"It was full of some sleeping dope," she said. "It would have been dangerous."

"Are you absolutely mad?"

"No."

"You had it *analyzed!*" He didn't believe it. His face showed.

"Yes."

"Why?"

"Because I—" Mandy stuck and pushed over a barrier—"saw her knock it over on purpose."

"Who?"

"Ione."

"*Ione!*"

"She—" Mandy stopped. "I saw her in the window glass," she said weakly. "Just—be careful."

"You're prepared to prove all this, I suppose," he said rather bleakly, in a moment.

"I— The handkerchief got burned up by mistake, but—"

"I see. I'm to take your word for it." His face hardened. "I had begun to think you were making sense," he told her crisply, "but I see your mind runs to melodrama. I think you'd better leave as soon as you politely can."

Mandy said, "Very well."

"I warned you the other night. You are not to worry my father."

"I haven't—"

"But you will," he said. "You're bound to." His lip curled. She saw, now, how angry he was. But he said, almost patiently, "You can't just walk into people's houses and stir up their lives, you know, to suit your appetite for a sensation."

"I'm sorry you don't believe me."

He ignored this. "My father is not a man who thrives on this sort of thing. Alarms and suspicions. He has been very kind and more than polite to you." His patient explanatory tone was unbearably insulting. "But he must have peace and I don't propose to let you attach yourself and your kind of imagination to his household."

"But it's true!" she cried. "It's true about the poison!"

He ignored it. "I believe you wanted my father to look at your work. He has looked at it. I think that's as far as you go."

Mandy was too furious to be meek any longer. "I think that's quite as far as I want to go," she blazed at him.

He seemed to have heard something elsewhere in the house. He held up his hand. He looked at her warily, without anger, with worse. "Don't make a scene," he said coldly.

Mandy drew herself up in tight control. "At least I've warned you," she said in a low voice. She turned to her pictures, her whole air that of departure.

He said, close behind her, "Excuse me if I sound stern. But you are rather a fantastic character, you know." He didn't sound angry at all, but as if he'd put her down as a type in his mind and was rather sorry for her. "I doubt whether you're even the wrong child, as you put it. I wouldn't be surprised if you'd dreamed yourself into that story. I'll bet you did, didn't you? Where did you hear it?"

She turned to face him, to protest.

Ione was in the archway. "Hello, there." She stepped briskly down. "How are you, my dear? Have you been here long? Have you had tea?" She loosened her black coat. Thone sprang to take it from her. "Thank you, dear. Thone, will you tell Elsie? Tea. Toby's on the phone?" She looked from one to the other and said cheerily, "You haven't been quarreling, children?"

"Oh, no," said Mandy with a stiff smile. "I was just about to go."

"Don't go. Toby will be in. He will be hurt if you run away. We must have tea, of course." Ione sat down and crossed her neat plump ankles. "I've been to see your mother," she said placidly. "That is, I was in her office this morning."

Thone, with her coat in his hands, turned suddenly back.

Mandy said, aghast, "You were!"

"Your real mother," said Ione, nodding pleasantly. "We had such a pleasant chat. A lovely person."

"It's the same woman?" asked Thone. "She was in that hospital?"

Ione said, "Oh, yes. But, my dear," she turned a pitying smile on Mandy, "how could you have imagined any such nonsense? Your mother hasn't the slightest doubt. The circumstances were quite clear, she says. There is no ground for error, really. Could you have misunderstood her, Amanda?"

Thone said grimly, "Amanda has quite an active imagination."

"So Mrs. Garth implied," said Ione, nodding. "And the child has been quite intense about painting. Mrs. Garth thinks that's the root of it. And perhaps it is." She spoke as if Amanda weren't there in the room at all.

Thone made a skeptical sound.

"You must remember," said Ione serenely, "that Toby is, after all, rather a glamorous figure. To a young artist, especially." She tilted her head. "Also, there are his scholarships. Oh, it's understandable." She beamed in her jolly way. "But, of course, we must have no more of it."

"I agree to that," Thone said quietly. "In fact, I've just said so." He went away with the coat.

Ione took off her white ruffled hat and set it beside her. Pink fingers touched her coiffure. "Your mother tells me that you have been well brought up. And I'm sure of that, my dear. I'm sure you won't come again if I find it best to suggest . . ." Her shoulders trembled in a little shrug. Her dark eyes were calm.

Mandy's heart pumped in slow surges. Her throat felt dry. After this, she could not come, ever again. They were cutting her out, both of them. Thone, perhaps, could be defied, but not the mistress of the house. It was perfectly clear and perfectly final. And humiliating beyond anything she had ever known. She would simply have to go.

But Thone hadn't believed her! Not a word she'd said! Would he be careful? Could she go and never come back and writhe every night in the silent hours, or sit up, heart drained with that wave of fear, sick with it, and helpless? Could she take her hurt feelings now and go home, muttering that her duty was done in the matter? And never blame herself?

No. She had botched it. So she was not excused.

Nor was he even temporarily safe, not now. Not after Kate had made it so plain, and removed from Ione any confusion whatsoever.

What if she accused Ione straight out? It couldn't be done.

She had nothing to go on. They wouldn't believe it. Why should they believe it?

She looked at Ione, so smug and sure, so much in control, so firm, such a little—what? Mandy's breathing came unevenly. Did she even believe it herself?

Tobias came in with Thone. He had heard no rumbles of wrath. He was, as he had been, Amanda's friend. Her very old friend and now her new friend, as well.

He showed Ione her pictures. Ione had little to say, but she listened cheerfully, as they all listened to his talk about them. Elsie brought tea. It was, for the artist, a pleasant afternoon that would end pleasantly. For Amanda it would end, indeed.

He was saying, "You seem to care about space and depth. But here, d'ya see? You have not placed the figure. The table is in space and the things on it, to a degree. But not the woman's head. See . . . here . . . that's a mere frame. What's *there?*"

Amanda followed his stabbing finger. Puzzled, she began to draw her brows together. Then almost without volition, so directly did the impulse pass into act, she did something different. She closed her eyes, she dropped her head, she put her palms along her cheeks, with finger tips at her temples. Unseeing, she listened to the silence and her heart surging. She kept remembering how Fanny had done it. She summoned her powers, dropped her hands, lifted her face, opened her smiling eyes, all in that smooth and vividly remembered rhythm. She said, as Belle used to say, "I see!"

She did see . . . a little trailing uneasiness cross the artist's face. She could feel the freezing of Thone's body, the deepening immobility of his attention.

So she drew up her knees and clasped her hands around them, then crossed her ankles and balanced, back straight. . . . "Tell me what else." She heard Thone mutter something, felt him lean forward. Tobias Garrison's hand trembled. That fine hand, retreating from the pointing gesture . . . surely it trembled a little. Even Ione's mouth—did it go slack? She hung onto the pose. Fanny had done this. She copied a copy. Maybe it was good enough.

Tobias sank back in the chair. Amanda turned to look and saw that Thone's eyes were very bright and rather startled. She unlocked her hands and stood up, trying to be all grace. She turned her foot. . . . She said, contritely, "I've taken too much time. I've tired you. You've been wonderful, Mr. Garrison. But I'd better go now."

"Don't—don't go, child," Tobias said. "For just a moment you looked—you seemed—I had a flash. Thone?"

"Yes," said Thone, very quietly, and it was exactly as if he went to stand behind his father, to put his shoulder at his father's back. "I saw what you meant, Dad."

"Saw what?" said Ione rather irritably.

"So—like Belle," said Tobias gently. "Something . . . just then."

"But that's not possible!" said Ione, deep in her throat.

Mandy agreed. "Oh, no, really. How could I be anything like that lovely creature?" She sounded rather breathless, as if she protested just a little too much. "I must say good-by. And thank you. I won't see you again."

"Why not?" said Tobias in surprise. "Of course you'll come again."

Amanda shook her head. Real tears came to her eyes and surprised her.

"My dear," said Tobias very earnestly, "I would like very much to see you at work. I know, even now, some tricks you should be told. I could, perhaps, guide you the way you're going. Why do you say you won't come back?" He was standing, now, very close to her. He liked her very much indeed. His interest was real. He wanted to help her. And Mandy responded. She wanted this, too. It wasn't a part of the other business. It was between them and it was real.

She said, reluctantly, showing the pain it was to withdraw, "You've been so kind. But I couldn't possibly ask you to bother any more."

"Why not?" said Tobias. He took hold of her shoulders and looked into her face. "See here, Amanda Garth, in the name of what we can't help thinking—for after all, you 'might have been'—you mustn't be shy with me. Must she, Thone?" It was as if he sensed that she'd had a rebuff from that quarter and turned to pin it down.

Thone said lightly, "If you want her, Dad, you sell her. Use your charm." He grinned at Tobias. He sent no messages to Mandy. He was, she felt, being very cautious.

Amanda said, "I haven't been shy at all, sir. I've been just the opposite. I want to confess and beg your pardon for the—" her lips quivered—"wild imagining I've done. I hadn't any right to. Mother was clear about it. It's as you say—I couldn't help thinking. And if you want to imagine something, of course, you always can." Smiling, he let her go.

"I'm so c-clever at it," she said. "I even told myself my father would have spared my mother. He wouldn't have wanted her to be uncertain. You see how wacky . . . ?" Mandy let her face break into a tearful smile. She tipped up her chin. Her head went back. There was no sound to her laughter.

She heard Thone's breath whistle as he drew it in. She let go the laughter and looked as innocently as she could at all their faces. Tobias' was fond. It wore a gentle radiance that was in some part sadness, yet not all.

He said, "Ah, but John Garth was just the man who would have spared her any doubt, had there been doubt. So it's not quite wacky, Amanda." He patted her shoulder.

Thone's face was a mask.

"I think I shall claim you both," Tobias said. "Please promise you'll come again."

Ione's dark eyes, turned upward, were wide. Then the muscles around them tugged and narrowed them the merest trifle. She said, parting her lips first, as if to smile, "My dear, by all means. Come again. You will, won't you?" Amanda looked straight at her. "Please promise," said Ione.

"I'd like to very much," said Mandy with a rush of relief. She thought to herself, Did it! Did it! I've confused her! She was filled with momentary triumph. Her feet took little dancing steps and she collected her belongings. She said rather jauntily to Thone, "Are you going back East soon?" It was in her mind to let him guess that her pretenses were temporary, to excuse herself, to explain. It was in her mind, but she knew at once it wasn't working. He guessed nothing of the kind. He hadn't believed a word she'd said. He didn't know what she was up to. There was no way he could understand. And his face was stony.

Tobias, for some reason, was quite gay. "Yes, so he intends, Amanda, and all the more reason why I should have some young life in the house. You must plan to come and stay over a day or two. You and I have studying to do. Tell her, Ione."

Ione said, "But of course, Amanda," in a singing tone.

"I may not go," said Thone uneasily.

His father looked surprised. Then he said happily, "My dear boy, wonderful! So much the better!"

9.

When Amanda had gone, Tobias came back into the studio with a little smile still on his lips.

Ione had withdrawn, as if she crept into a deep corner of her chair. She sat still and she did not speak. Tobias put a warm hand on Thone's shoulder. It said to Thone, "My son." Thone looked up quickly. "I'm not worried about that," his face said. "Never think it."

All this the woman could not read.

Tobias said aloud, "That's a darling girl."

"Damnedest thing," said Thone. He got out of his chair and took a pace or two. "You realize, Dad, that kind of mannerism can't be inherited." Tobias shrugged. "Not that I ever heard," muttered Thone. "Science would be astonished. Darn funny thing! Matter of fact, it's uncanny. Look here, Dad, you don't suppose we really were changed around, swapped in the cradle, hm?" His eyes weren't worried. They were amused.

"I never thought so," said Tobias mildly.

"I hope you checked."

"I'm no logician, no worker-out of puzzles, no sorter of evidence and drawer of conclusions therefrom," said Tobias half humorously. "But this Garth, the father, he was, you see."

"*He* settled it?"

"Seemed clear as crystal at the time." Tobias went and stood looking off toward the mountains. "Nice fellow, Garth. Very clear in the head." His voice was indulgent.

Thone's mouth twisted. "Science is a wonderful thing, all the same," he murmured. There were overtones in their talk. Ione had no ear for them.

Tobias jingled coins in his pocket. "Interesting girl," he said dreamily. "How she happens to . . . remind us of Belle, we'll never know. But that doesn't disturb me. I know you're afraid it will. Don't be afraid. I like her, damn it!"

"You've got a right," said Thone, quickly and generously. He took a pace or two, frowning. "Beats me. Wasn't an illusion, if we both got it."

Tobias said dreamily, "That's a lovely face. Mouth. Notice the mouth?"

"Um, yes," said Thone, "I noticed the mouth."

"I'd like to paint it," the artist said. Thone's eyes glinted, perhaps with humor.

The woman got no overtones. She sat, smoldering. Her small rosy fingers drew on the chair arm a slow design.

She said suddenly, aloud, "The week-end?"

"Eh?"

"I was thinking," she said, "it would be nice to have her over the week-end." She laced her fingers. "There are people coming in, Saturday. A little party. So nice for Amanda. Besides, she must come before Thone has to leave us."

"Ask her," Tobias murmured.

She nodded and nodded. "Yes. Yes, I shall call this evening. Such an interesting girl, as you say, Toby. We must see more of her." She rolled her thumbs against each other. "And I do believe the child said it was her vacation? It should work out very well."

"She may have other plans for her vacation." Thone's voice was empty of expression.

Ione's hands parted in a brushing gesture. She wiggled herself out of the chair. "Toby, dear," she cried, "I shall ask her for a week, at least. Oh, yes, I think so. If you have studying to do," she went on firmly, smilingly, insistently, "a day or two is not enough to learn much, is it?"

"True. True." Tobias smiled, jingling the coins.

Thone sat down and opened a magazine and put his gaze on it.

"Thone! You lamb! Come in. And me not in my best complexion yet. Why didn't you warn me to make myself beautiful?"

"'Tain't ever necessary, Fanny darling." He kissed her.

"Blarney. Blarney. Come and sit. Talk to me." Fanny bustled him into a chair. "I have to go to work this afternoon. What a pity! You and I might have gone to the zoo or something. Is there anything wrong?"

"How quick you are!" said Thone admiringly. "No sooner is my foot in the door than you see all, know all."

She brought him cigarettes and matches. "It's that girl, I'll bet. That Amanda girl."

"I said you knew." His face was too somber to suit her. Fanny sat down on her sofa, her back beautifully straight.

"Fanny, darling," said he, "I can't understand this Amanda. Can you? She's the strangest combination. One minute, I think this is a fine, intelligent, sensitive—"

"So it is," said Fanny.

"What?"

"She was here, day before yesterday. We talked."

"Ah," said Thone.

"Go on."

"Where were we?"

"Fine, intelligent . . ."

"Oh, yes. And then, again, I'm convinced that she's crazy."

"What makes you think she's crazy?"

"She says somebody wants to poison me."

"Thone!"

"That's what she said, unless I failed to hear properly. Did she mention that little item to you?"

"God's grief! No!"

"Also," said Thone, "does she think she's my father's daughter? Or doesn't she?"

"There I can't help, because I can't tell. Thone, dear, I think she's tempted."

"You talked it over?"

"Not exactly. This is how it was. You see, I told her a good bit about all of you. I'm frank to say, I liked the girl. I felt she took quite a beating the other night, what with Ione being so grim and cryptic, and Toby having a spell. She's terribly interested, Thone. That's natural. She listens well. Perhaps," she made a face, "I let myself go"

"You told her about my mother and—the divorce from Ione. All that?"

"Yes. All that. Do you mind?"

"No," he said. "Ione is asking her up for a week." His hands fell a little helplessly.

"Um-hum," Fanny prodded.

"Dad fell for her. And you know Ione. Anything Dad wants."

"Is she coming?"

"I don't know. If she does, Fanny, after yesterday—I am confused."

"What about yesterday?"

He rubbed his hand through his hair. "She was at the house in the afternoon. First, of course, I was afraid she'd upset Dad. You know how it struck him the other night."

"Belle's death, dear. It always does."

"Yes, I know. I didn't want anything like it to happen again. I made it a point to be around."

"Yes?"

"Well, Dad fell for her, as I said. They—it was fine. But the minute he turned his back, she was at me with this wild poison business." Fanny shook her head in bewilderment.

"I don't know what that was all about, nor do I much care," said Thone impatiently. "I don't know what to think. The part that's really got me going in circles . . . Yesterday she did some things—in Belle's image!" Fanny moved her lashes. "It was damned queer! Dad and I both . . . Now how the hell? You can't inherit, for instance, a way to sit, a habit of closing her eyes to think . . ."

"Or," said Fanny, "for instance, a laugh!" She rose. She towered in anger. "Or a way of standing!" she cried. "Or a gesture like this?"

His scalp seemed to move as he stared at her.

"*My* little tricks! *My* memories!" she shrilled. "Oh, the sly! The cruel! The devil!"

"She got them from you!"

"Of course she did! Of course she did!"

"I'll wring her neck," said Thone simply. He was halfway to the door. "Where does she live? Where can I find her?"

"Wait."

"Do you know?"

"I know. I'll tell you, directly. Wait a minute." Fanny was calmer. She came toward him. Her old face was filled with her love for him. "Don't wring any necks, Thone. Please wait. Subside! Subside!" She flailed at him with her hands. "She's a nice girl, Thone. I couldn't be so fooled."

"She's not a nice girl. She fooled me, too."

"What do you think?"

"She's trying to make us believe she is Belle's daughter. She wants to be. Prestige. Maybe it's money."

"Oh," said Fanny, "not money."

"Don't be naive, Fanny."

"Thone, honey, go there. Find out. But easy, easy," she crooned. "You must do exactly what your impulse is. Get to the bottom of it. But do it some easy way, please, for Fanny."

"You fell for her too," he accused.

"She's a darling," said Fanny. "So help me, God and all my experience. Besides, you're bigger than she is. She's not your size."

"I won't beat her," said Thone, with a smile struggling for his

mouth. "You're an old incorrigible darling yourself. I'll go easy."
His jaw hardened. "Where?"

She got him a piece of paper. "There," she said. Her head followed him out the door. "And you'll let me know?" said Fanny, big-eyed, brilliant with curiosity.

Kate opened the door. She wore a house dress. Her fair hair, streaked with gray, was bound back in a plain fashion from her plain face. There was a heaviness around her eyes.

"Does Amanda Garth live here?"

"She does. She's not here at the moment."

"Where can I find her?" he asked sternly.

"She's just gone to market. It's her Easter vacation. Will you wait?"

"Are you Mrs. Garth?"

"I am."

"My name is Garrison."

Kate's eyes winced at the name. "Come in," she said. The living room of this little cottage was cool and yet bright. The furnishings were informal and inexpensive, but the lines were good and the arrangement spoke of taste. Kate said, "Sit down, won't you? I'm not normally at home on Wednesdays myself. I—had a bad night."

"I'm sorry," he said, more gently than he had intended. "I think my stepmother came to see you yesterday."

"Yes." Kate didn't pick up that subject to carry it further. She was distressed by it. She hadn't liked talking to Ione at her office yesterday. She hadn't enjoyed having to say, or as much as say, that she was ashamed of Mandy. She wasn't going to like having to say it again to this very good-looking young man, who was pretty angry, although not with her. He was excepting Kate from his anger with fine control. He sat down. He had fine blue eyes, as blue as Mandy's, as blue as her own.

"My stepmother called here last evening. Does Amanda intend to accept that invitation?"

Kate drew in a quick breath. Her eyes went out of focus as she looked past him. Ione had been so generous with cordial patter on the telephone last evening. "Dear Mrs. Garth, you will let her come. . . ." But there hadn't been a right *feel* to the whole incident. And nothing had seemed right, either, about Mandy's face, when she had taken the phone herself.

Mandy saying. "It's so sweet of you. It would be lovely. . . . Why, I'd love to, Mrs. Garrison, if you're sure . . . Of course, it would be. . . . You're kind. . . ." Mandy's lips curved but not smiling. Mandy's eyes very wide and staring. Mandy's voice gushing just a little too much, saying, "*May* I call you tomorrow, *please*, Mrs. Garrison? I would *so* love to come, but I'm not quite sure . . ." Mandy saying, "Oh, thank you. Yes, I will. Yes, indeed, I will." Mandy closing her eyes, as the phone went to its cradle, with that odd, odd curve on her mouth.

Kate had asked, "Are you going?"

"Oh, I'll think about it."

Kate still heard that false flip answer, the tap of Mandy's heels off to the kitchen, where she had finished the dishes.

And in the muscles of her back she could still feel the stiff silence of last evening. For although they had chatted, they had said no more.

"Does she?" repeated Thone.

Kate's eyes came back, full of pain. "I don't really know," she said. "I can't tell you."

But Thone was looking at her now as if he had lost his place in the conversation. "Do you realize," he said irrelevantly, and almost impishly, "that if there had been a switch of infants, you'd be my mother?"

The little smile lines around Kate's eyes cut into her fair skin. Her long droll face expressed a comical consternation. He grinned. "What a horrible thought!" He trusted her to know he didn't mean it. "Seriously, Mrs. Garth . . ."

She was quickly serious. She looked down at her big strong hands. "Mandy is mine," she said quietly, "and knows that."

"*Does* she, though?"

"Of course she does."

"O.K. She knows." His anger was close to the surface again. "Then what is she trying to do?"

"I don't know," said Kate. "I'm very much upset about it. I do not know. She—evades me. She never has, until now. So I can't . . . You must talk to Mandy."

"That's what I intend to do," he said, gentled again by her unhappiness.

Kate turned her hand in rather a helpless gesture. "She wants to paint. . . ."

"I understand that much."

Kate lifted her head. "I think there must be a reason. I'm beginning to be sure of that. Mandy wouldn't do this sort of thing unless she had a reason."

"Because," said Thone oddly, "she's such a darling?"

Kate looked startled. "Yes," she said, rather snappishly.

"And everybody loves her?" he drawled.

"Everybody should," said Kate. Disloyalty was a bad taste in her mouth. She had the sensation of spitting it out.

"I'm sorry, Mrs. Garth," said Thone, wilting into plain bewilderment. "I'm upset, too. I don't understand what's in her mind. Is it just, do you think, that she's young and silly?"

"Your age," said Kate, tossing it back at him. Thone kept his eyes on hers. Suddenly they liked each other enormously.

Amanda whirled in like a small dusty tornado. She wore the old blue pants and old huaraches and a plaid shirt, and she had a big brown paper bag of stuff in her arms, which she balanced, in part, by the use of her chin. She said, "Oh!" She was gone into the kitchen and back again, without the bag, in another whirl. She looked like a fairly ragged little boy. She stood in the middle of the room and stared at Thone with stormy eyes.

"I'm glad you came," she said. "I have a few things to say to you."

He got out of the chair in which the speed of her entrance had surprised him. He got up, now, very slowly, rather ominously. He loomed very large. Mandy's head went back to follow him up, but she stood her ground. The space between them was sultry. Thin currents of antagonism seemed to eddy and threaten in the heated air.

Kate said sharply, "I think I'll leave you."

"No, Mother. It's hot," said Mandy quickly. "We'll go out back. Come on." She yanked her head at Thone. Her eyes were like lightning.

"I'm coming," he said, as mild as the dull distant promise of thunder on the horizon.

It was hot in the back yard. Mandy marched all the way back to the olive tree and faced him in the shade. But he stole the advantage. His voice was crisp and clear, not muddied with his anger, but the deep anger lashed like a whip, just the same.

"Why did you imitate my mother, as Fanny taught you?"

She put her hands behind her back. "Go on," she said. "Ask all the questions and then I'll tell you the answers."

"What are you trying to do to my father? If you know you are not his child, why do you pretend you are, with your hands and feet and eyes, while your mouth says, 'Oh, no'? Part of you is a liar! Why?"

"Go on," she said saucily.

"Do you intend to come and stay in that house?"

"That depends."

"On what?"

"On you."

"I'm glad you have some pride."

"Pride!" said Mandy.

"What kind of—"

"Why don't you ask me," she interrupted, "about the poison?"

"I don't believe in any poison," he said contemptuously.

She sighed. "That's why."

"Why what?"

"Why everything."

"I don't get it."

"*Because* you won't believe in any poison, I had to copy Fanny."

"This makes it clear?" he mocked.

"To me it does. If you're ready, I'll try to explain."

"Explain," he said.

"When I went up the first time," she fluttered, "it was just what I said. . . ." She flopped down cross-legged on the grass and put her face in her hands. "Now it's a mess," she moaned.

He sat down and leaned, half lying on his elbow. He plucked a grass stem. He waited with cold patience.

"You remember that we went down to your room? I happened to be looking into the window glass. It was like a mirror. She didn't know I could see her, but I did see her, perfectly. Your stepmother, Ione, knocked your thermos jug off onto the floor. I wondered, because she pretended that it was an accident. So I happened to get some of the chocolate on my handkerchief. I—I know a boy . . ."

"Naturally," said Thone rather dryly while she hesitated.

"I kept puzzling, you see? And he happens to be a chemist."

"So you had it analyzed," he said flatly.

"And it was loaded with sleeping dope."

"But you can't, now, produce the handkerchief," he said in the same tone.

"I can produce the man who analyzed it," she snapped.

"Who, no doubt, considers you a darling."

She stared at him. "I don't know why I don't let you go ahead and get poisoned."

Nothing changed in his face. "Yes, why don't you?" He reached for another blade of grass.

Mandy closed her eyes. Oh, God, she thought. Well, all right. It won't make any sense unless I tell him. All right. Let him have it. She said, painfully, fumbling her way to a confession, "You're probably used to having girls fall for you, with no encouragement." She opened her eyes. He was looking at her with a face so white and hurt and frightened that she stopped with her mouth open—just too late hearing with his ears the thing she'd said. "I'm s-sorry." Her face flooded with color. "I didn't mean—I was only trying to say—"

"Shall we skip this part?" He threw away his piece of grass. "Go back to where you had it analyzed."

"I tried to call you, as soon as I knew the stuff was dangerous. I couldn't get you on the phone. I went to Fanny Austin, to see if I could *understand* it."

"You didn't mention poison to her."

"No. Because, after that, I thought I knew. I guessed you were safe."

"Safe?" His eyebrows were unexcited and skeptical.

"For now," said Mandy. Her heart ached. She put her hands over it. "I know what it looked like to you. But the point is, as long as she's confused, you're safe. That's why I had to try to confuse her."

"Who?"

"Ione."

"What's Ione got to do with it?"

"I think she wanted you to die."

"You're crazy!" he exploded.

"Maybe," said Mandy, troubled. "Anyhow, now that I've had this chance to tell you the whole thing, I can stay out of it. You can look after yourself. I don't really want to come up and stay. I don't really want to upset your father."

He shook his head. "I'm not sure "I'm getting this. Are you claiming to have been protecting *me?*"

"Of course," said Mandy.

"From sudden death?" She nodded. He let himself fall flat on his back and roared.

She waited silently.

"So Ione was going to kill me off?" He sat up and brushed off grass. His eyes were still brimming with bitter mirth. They hunted her serious face as if to confirm the joke. "Why?" he demanded. "What's she got against me?"

"You're Belle's child."

"Oh, come."

"Only she's not quite sure of that, right now."

"Not sure?"

"That *you're* Belle's child. She thinks maybe it's me."

"You don't know what you are saying," he said in a minute, rather pityingly. "You don't know what it's all about."

"There was poison," said Mandy slowly, stubbornly, "in your chocolate."

"If there was, Ione *destroyed* it."

Mandy shook her head. "Then was it your father? Or the servants? Or Fanny? Who wanted you to die?"

"Nobody wants me to die," he said, "as far as I know."

"But there was poison and she knew it." Mandy clenched her fists. "Tell me this: Did you ever have a narrow escape before?"

He kept looking at her and his face sobered, subtly. "Anyone has accidents."

"But you did? Where? Here?" He shrugged and she struck at his arm. "Tell me!"

"Damned near got electrocuted in the bathroom once," he admitted cheerfully. "What of it?"

"Here?" He nodded. Their eyes clung a moment. Mandy put her knees up and her head on them. "That settles it," she said in a muffled voice.

"It hardly settles anything." His voice was hard. "You've worked up quite a complicated story out of nothing much. There's one thing that is settled, however. Whatever reason you think you've got, you'll ape my mother no more!"

"No?" She straightened angrily. "You mean you still don't believe there was any poison? But why should I say so? Why should I lie?"

"Why do you do anything?" he murmured. "I think you're fond of plots."

"How did your mother die?" she flung at him. "Where was Ione then?"

"That's enough." He got to his feet.

"You were there, weren't you?" She scrambled up. She was pleading. "Don't you see? Ione must have hated your mother. Don't you see how this could be part of the same . . ."

He looked down, inscrutably, brushing off grass.

"But how do you know?" she wailed. "What makes you so sure it wasn't murder?"

"So now," he said icily, "your marvelous intuition knows better than the police investigation, the doctors, the husband, the son, and all who were alive and present six years ago."

"But *is* it impossible?"

"Yes," he said. "It's impossible." His eyes blazed. "And if you ever breathe one syllable, one hint, of any such notion to my father, I will wring your neck. Do you realize—is your cheap mind capable of realizing what you'd do to him? You'd kill him! You'd tear him to pieces! You shut your ignorant mouth! You keep your nose out of my father's memories, or by God, I'll—"

He'd grabbed her in his fury. He was going to shake her. She hung in his grasp.

"So I'll shut my mouth and you'll get murdered!" she cried. Her head snapped back as he lifted her in anger. She began to cry. But she paid no attention to her tears and they rolled down her face. "Of course I won't say it to your father! What do you think I— Let me go! I promise. I promise that."

He let her go.

She staggered back, rubbing her shoulder, and the tears kept flowing. "I wouldn't hurt your father."

"All right," said Thone.

There was a long minute of silence under the tree. Sun and shade played nervously on their faces. She said in a low voice, "Will you leave there? Will you go away?"

"No."

She crossed her arms, still feeling the bruises. "Then I can't help it. I'll have to do it. Have to. Because I'm the only one in the world who can."

He moistened his lips. "Do what?"

"Come up there," said Mandy, flaming at him, "and walk into your place. All right! Since you won't believe it, suppose you pull up a chair and watch her try to murder me!"

10.

He sank, after a shocked moment, down on the grass again. Mandy crouched, peering at his face. "Have I convinced you?" she dared at last.

He passed a hand over his eyes and looked at her wearily. "I beg your pardon," he said, "for coming so near to beating you, after all." She brushed this off with a little movement of her head. "You've convinced me of one thing," he said wryly. "*You* are convinced about it."

She said, "And I do—love your father."

"Yes, I—" His eyes fled from hers. "What am I going to do with you?" he murmured.

Mandy wiped her face on her sleeve and sniffled. "Let it go the way it is. Look," she said with an air of great reasonableness, "what can the harm be in letting her think we were mixed up? When we were born? And just see. If I'm right there'll have to be something."

"What about Dad?"

"He'll never believe you're not his son," said Mandy promptly. "Will it hurt him to claim us both for a little while?"

"It'll hurt your mother," he surprised her by saying.

"Yes."

"Will you explain to her?"

"To Mother? Can't."

"I don't agree with you."

"She wouldn't let me near that house. Ever again. Can't tell her."

"She'd understand," said Thone stubbornly.

"Of course she would," flared Mandy. "But my mother loves *me*. She'd want *me* safe. Don't you see?"

He was silent a long moment. "Why, yes," he said at last, not looking up. "I guess I see." He put his palm flat on the grass. "Suppose I say no?"

"Then," said Mandy, "I'll maybe have to go to the police."

He caught his breath but he didn't say anything. "You don't take it seriously enough to be careful," she wailed. "I couldn't trust you to be careful. And I have to sleep nights. Samaritan type," she added flippantly.

"All right," he said suddenly, meeting her gaze with grave eyes. "As long as you don't upset my father."

"It would upset him quite a lot, I think," said Mandy quietly, "if you should die."

He gave in, let something go. "Obviously, you'll have to be up there." She nodded.

"I think she wants to watch me. I think she's puzzled. I—really think so."

"I know you think so," he said.

They sat in silence a moment, a strangely peaceful silence. She didn't know, couldn't guess what he was thinking. She stirred.

"Maybe you could help push it along. Let her suppose *you* think I'm the real child."

"It's ridiculous," he said lightly, "but have it your way, on my conditions." There was something faintly suggesting mischief in his eye, something a trifle warmer, a mere hint that he, too, might like to watch her. "I hope you realize we are almost certainly going to prove you've been having nightmares."

"Just so they stop," she said, lightly, too. "What about Fanny Austin? She mustn't tell Ione how I was faking."

"I'll see she doesn't," he said, rather absently. In a moment he got to his feet. And she rose also. "Shall we tell your mother? What shall we tell her?"

"You just say good-by," said Mandy with a funny little twinge of jealousy. "I'll tell her something or other."

They went in, and Kate, searching their faces, saw that the storm had passed, having, apparently, done no damage. Thone took Kate's hand to say good-by. That was all he said. "Good-by, Mrs. Garth." But it wasn't all that passed between them. Mandy chewed on her lip. Her Kate! She felt outraged and at the same time enlightened. How it must feel, for Thone, when Tobias so plainly liked her! She said good-by to him rather humbly.

Then, when the house was empty of his presence, when it seemed to sigh and let go at its seams, Mandy turned. "You liked him, Mother." It was more accusation than question.

"Yes, I did," said Kate calmly.

"I am going up there. I'm going to accept. I'm going Friday."

Kate's eyes came up, waiting to be hurt. Mandy plunked herself on the floor at her feet, "Mamma," she said, leaning her head childishly on Kate's knee, "now you've seen him, I would like to state that I'm in love with that guy. I don't think he's interested. But—a Garth doesn't give up—so soon, hm?"

She heard her mother's breath stop, catch, and go on. Kate's hand pushed down through her hair, rough with her quick response. "Sic 'em, babe," said Kate shakily. And Mandy turned her face and howled into her mother's skirt.

Gene said, "You're going up there Friday, for a week, huh? And I can't have any dates! Fine thing!"

"Well, but Gene, I'll be their house guest."

"Who's they? This Garrison's the artist, the one who's going to learn you art. And—?"

"His wife and his son."

"Son," said Gene. "About how old?"

"Oh, Gene . . ."

"Mandy, don't kid me."

"O.K. He's twenty-three and very attractive."

"Yeah," said Gene. "Art." He lit a cigarette. "Listen, remember that handkerchief? Did that have anything to do with this Garrison bunch?"

"Well, yes, it did."

"Don't you go, Mandy."

"But it's all right!"

"How do you know?"

"Gene," she said earnestly, "you'll have to let me go the way I'm going."

His red-brown eyes were hurt for just a moment. Then he answered, "Sure, Mandy, if you say so," stoically. "But any time, say for instance you'd need a bodyguard . . ." He drew his forefinger along the back of her hand.

"I'll remember," said Mandy thoughtfully.

He squirmed. "You better," he said darkly.

Thone came for her on Friday afternoon, in the convertible. Mandy wore the cream-yellow suit, with her black shoes and bag, and a navy-blue blouse. When she saw that the top was down she tied a yellow scarf around her hair. Kate was at the office, so there was no one to whom she must say good-by. He took her suitcase and her paints. She locked the cottage door.

It was a bright afternoon, windy and clear. On all sides the hills were visible and sharp, cutting the flat land into valleys. The brilliant light picked out the brightest colors, greens in the landscape, red, orange, magenta flowers, and beat them to a sparkling blend. No color could be garish in this sun. Nor could there be too much color. The bright air consumed it all.

"What a day!" Mandy sparkled.

"Pretty windy," said Thone. "Will you be warm enough?"

"In this? Oh, yes."

"Same outfit you wore at the galleries," he said, astonishing her. "Did you bring those trousers?"

"N-no."

"Too bad." He put her things in the back. "Like to drive?" he said.

She gasped. "Oh, I'd love to! Do you mean you'll let me?"

"Hop in."

As he got in beside her, he passed a hand over his eyes. "Headache?" she said.

"No."

She found what to push and started the car and was charmed with the sensation of handling it. "It's Ione's car," he told her. "Too windy for Dad today. So they're off in his sedan."

"They're off?"

"They'll be home by the time we get there."

If this was an adventure, it felt, for now, like a gay one. The day, the car, the man who was here, no matter if his mood was remote, whose profile in the corner of her eye was so unaccountably satisfying . . . Mandy acquired confidence and drove with ease. In the breeze, a corner of the scarf whipped and vibrated back of her ear. They slid smoothly through Glendale. They topped a rise. And there the far mountains cut the sky, huge, silent, and clear.

"How beautiful they are today!"

"Chinese," said Thone.

"What?"

"Oh, I don't know. These views strike me . . ."

"Have you been in China much?"

"Some, during the war."

"Oh, but you did live out there, didn't you?"

"Yes, a long time. But a good ways from China. Hawaii for a while. Tahiti . . ."

"It must be . . . ummmm," she sighed. She thought of Belle, whose memory must be entwined with all those years. "Were you in the Army?" she asked, changing time.

"In a way," he said. "I had an awful time getting them to use me at all. Turned out I knew a few languages that were handy in the East. Lucky for me."

She said, "Oh, so you talked yourself into it?"

"Uh-huh," he smiled. "Talked me a good war. Jabbered myself right through it."

"Action?"

"No battles," he said shortly.

"Now you want to be an architect. Fanny told me."

"Fanny must have done a good bit of talking."

"I like her."

"Who could not?" he said briefly. "Yes, I'm trying to learn. Did Fanny tell you I can afford it?"

Mandy frowned. She didn't answer. A shadow crossed, not the bright scene, but her sense of it.

He said, "I beg your pardon."

She said lightly, "Yes, I think you might. However, she told me. You're lucky, aren't you? So am I."

"In what? How do you mean?" He turned to look at her.

Mandy's mouth had a sweet curve to it. "I'm studying, too. I have my chance. I think that's lucky."

"So it is," said Thone mildly, and they rode on. Later he said, "Don't turn yet. We'll have to take the lower road. You won't mind a little climb, will you? Up the garden? Ione keeps this thing in the lower garage."

Mandy's knuckles whitened where she gripped the wheel. "Just tell me where," she said, not quite controlling her voice.

He told her where to turn. They began to enter a fold of the mountain. The road was flat. The ground rose on either side, higher and steeper.

"I see," said Thone pleasantly, "that Fanny also told you how Belle died."

They had passed out of light into shadow as if the canyon

swallowed them. The shade, to sun-dazed eyes, was somber and shocking. Amanda shivered. Two or three houses, huddled at the roadside, backed against the slopes, odd in shape as if the terrain had forced them to eccentricity, as, indeed, it had. "I wouldn't care to live in these," she said, to cover the shuddering.

"There were no houses down here at all six years ago," said Thone. "No, I agree with you. I'd rather be up, and look over."

They came to a set of doors and a concrete apron. The flat-topped building was tucked into the steep side of the hill, almost, although not quite, like a cave. Thone said, "Here we are." She stopped the car, hesitantly. The doors were open, swung back and caught in a form of hook on either side.

The inner space looked very tiny. Bare, just a box, with a few steps at the back to a small door halfway up the wall. Thone said, "Run her in." She eased the long car in. "Good," he said. She set the brake and turned the key in sudden panic. The motor died.

He made no move to get out. "You're afraid of what I may be feeling, aren't you? Don't be."

"N-no, I—"

"This is where she died. Dad won't face it. They built another garage, squeezed it in up above. He can't come here. But I can."

"He must have adored her," said Mandy tremulously.

"And so did I." He was silent a moment and Mandy quivered with the wish that he'd go on, that he'd let himself tell her, and with the fear that she'd spoil it, with the sudden thrill of being so near to being near him.

"I figure," said Thone quietly, "that you needn't worry where you die. Death sanctifies. It's solemn enough to make its own shrine, wherever it happens. I thought that many times, during the war." He shifted his shoulders. "God knows it hurt me when Belle died, but I try to remember that it didn't hurt her. She fell asleep. If she slept all the way out, here, on this not very clean floor, why, something here is holy now. So I feel—just that. Do you see?"

"I'm pretty ignorant," said Mandy softly. "Please forgive me." She lay back and closed her eyes to catch the tears.

"But I've been thinking over what you suggested."

"Oh!"

"I couldn't help it. Well, you see, she'd had some chloral. It knocked her out. There was chloral around the house. She used to fix it for Dad. No one else touched it. That's why we think she got it by mistake."

Mandy opened her eyes. "But how could she? Doesn't it taste?"

"Sure does. But Belle liked a liqueur. Herbsaint. Ever have any? It's terrific. It's as strong a drink as you'd ever want to taste. She called it her firewater. She liked to roll it around on her—" He stopped and changed sentences quickly. "Well, she had some that night. She almost always did have a little after dinner in the evening. The only thing we could imagine was—somehow in the liqueur, she didn't notice, or . . ." He hesitated. "There wasn't a thing to help us, you know. The glasses we'd used—hers, Dad's, mine—I had a Coke—were washed and put away by the time we knew what had happened. Elsie and Burt came in about midnight. Dad never got out of his chair after dinner except once, to answer the phone. Nor did I. There wasn't another soul in the house."

Mandy shook her head.

"He fell asleep. I was reading. We were waiting for her." He roused himself suddenly and continued in a brisker voice. "Of course, long ago, I decided that she took it on purpose. Oh, no, not that! I mean, to get the effect that Dad gets. Dad takes his in milk. It doesn't knock him out. It makes him drowsy. But chloral in alcohol works like lightning. It must have worked like that with her. So, I wonder if her putting the stuff with alcohol wasn't the real accident. I don't suppose she thought of it as dangerous. I tell myself that's the way it was."

"Yes," said Mandy. Her throat hurt.

"One thing," said Thone. "I'm sure she didn't want to die."

"Oh, don't—don't. Don't tell me all this. Don't bring it all back. I'm sorry."

"Part of my treatment," said Thone gently. "I'm curing a delusion."

And Mandy's heart swooped, sank sickeningly. She said nothing. She tried to smile. But to herself, she thought, There is no delusion. There was poison in the chocolate.

He helped her out, closed the doors, barred them. The place was very dim after he had done so. They went up the steps and he opened the door at the top and let her through it to a kind of workshop and storeroom that sat against the hillside half a story above the garage. It was crammed with stuff, the kind of thing that accumulates in a garage, and it was lit, rather eerily, by a broad band of glass brick, high on the back wall, through which they could not see. Thone crossed this place to another door and used a key from the key case to unlock it. They emerged on the first of a series of terraces.

Here they stood above the garage, yet far below the house, which she could see now, ugly and rather terrifying from this strange angle. The hillside garden was shut in by a wall, a wall that traveled almost vertically and had to do so in steps and angles.

Thone said, "That wall just about kills me. Isn't it ugly? Dad had it built last fall to protect his privacy. It's mad, isn't it? Somebody crept up the back way a couple of times to gawk at him. Now the only way in from below is through the garage and all those doors. Nuisance." He threw the keys up and caught them again. "Got your breath? Come on."

So they rose from terrace to terrace, sometimes by a short flight of steps, sometimes by a rambling path that took hairpin curves. They wound slowly upward to come at last to a door in the bottom level of the house.

The guest room was on this level. Thone said maybe she'd like to know that Elsie and Burt had their quarters on this level also. "It's pretty weird, I know. Feels like the house was pressing you down. But you aren't isolated. Must you—wash or anything?"

"No," said Mandy, sweeping the odd-shaped room, the door to a bath with one fierce glance. "Let's get on with it, shall we?" She thought to herself, I'll get on with it. He isn't with me. Nobody is. If there is any evil in this house, I'm all alone against it.

11.

Tobias was more than cordial. It wasn't long before Mandy began to feel that the situation she had herself set up was developing with breathless speed, leaping and bounding and running away from her. For Tobias engulfed her. They talked for hours. Or, rather, he talked, spilling out thoughts and ideas, observations and theories that tumbled forth in cascades, in floods, as if they'd been dammed up too long. Mandy was fascinated. Receptive, charmed, excited, she listened and learned. Thone was there, receptive also to his father's thought, but oddly remote from Mandy. They made an unfinished triangle. Tobias at the apex. The base line between the boy and girl not drawn.

As for Ione, she came and went. She ran the house around them. She was like the captain of a ship, who kept the vessel on its physical course while they, the passengers, rode on the winds of the mind, scarcely noticing how their bodies were carried.

Saturday was the same. All morning, in the studio, Tobias was wound up and spun on. He was almost feverishly happy.

Mandy had no private words with Thone. She'd scarcely seen old Elsie, and her husband, Burt, was only a bent figure in the gardens. She'd scarcely spoken to Ione.

Ione, who came and went. Who listened, sometimes. Sometimes not. Who, when she joined in, brought the talk down lumpishly. Amanda knew, now, what Fanny had meant. Ione couldn't spin, spurning the earth on wide wings of abstractions. Somehow she always came to a detail. She was bounded, shrewd and capable, busy and small, but lacking a dimension.

Did she watch, though? Mandy didn't know. She hadn't had time; she was dizzy.

They snatched a supper, Saturday, because there was going to be an evening party. People were coming in. Mandy must dress up a bit, they told her.

Down in her room, at the bottom of the house, she creamed her face and bathed and breathed a little. She suffered, in this space of self-communion, an attack of honest doubt.

If Ione did not like her, if there was no warmth, no welcome, it was far from surprising. Here I come, thought Mandy, and Tobias just goes overboard. I walk in here and take him over. And am barely polite to her, my hostess. I don't even try to take her into the talk. I sit and goggle at him and he loves it. Of course he would. I'm young and I do understand what he says and I lap it all up. If she feels like murdering me, no wonder! Thone, too. How can he possibly like me? Adores his father. But here come I . . .

Mandy looked into her own troubled eyes in the glass. But I didn't mean to. She begged her own pardon. The eyes in the glass refused it. "You'd better git for home, Amanda Garth," they said. "Now that you see yourself, it isn't pretty, is it?"

She went up to the party. She wore a pale satin frock. It was an icy green. It fell off her shoulders demurely, and it billowed in shining folds below her knees. But the cut at her hips and breast was not demure. She'd brushed her short hair back from her ears. She wore no jewelry, not even a flower, nothing to break the shimmering lines.

Tobias put both hands out. "Ah, here's my girl! Here's Amanda! Lovely . . . lovely . . . Isn't she lovely?" Her hands in his, Amanda was drawn forward.

"Lovely indeed!" said one of his cronies reverently.

"This— You say your daughter!" squeaked another, touching his eyeglasses.

"I only say she might have been," Tobias glowed.

"I say, Toby, you're going to paint that—er—face, of course?"

"If she'll sit," said the artist fondly. "She's not a model, George. She is herself a painter."

"Inherited your genius, too, eh?"

"Oh, no," said Amanda. She turned to look for the guest who had spoken. She saw Fanny, in white and silver, flip a greeting from another group. Then she saw Ione.

Ione, the little lady, the hostess, the chatelaine. Plump and neat in her sleeved beige gown that was folded at the bosom. Sleek and sedate, white hair meticulously coiffed, brows brushed, cheeks rosy and with a faint frost of powder. Lips smiling. Perhaps it was the hostess's smile, pasted on, concealing a mind full of lists and tasks. But the dark eyes, which should have been darting and taking notes and managing this roomful of people, were now, for this moment, fastened on the beauty in ice green. Nothing to be read in that fixed look. It was rather blank. It was rather blind.

Amanda looked away. She murmured something. Her eyes

hunted Thone. He was surrounded by three young women, a red-head who never took her eyes off him, a brunette who slouched this way and that, throwing her hips, and a silver blonde in a bouffant skirt, rolling her big eyes, stroking a long soft handkerchief that she held at the corner. Amanda's lips twitched. She thought, I resign. She let herself down, lowered her own pitch. She would sit this one out. She would retire.

So doing, she defeated her own purpose. For the decision gave her young beauty an uncanny poise. People buzzed around her. In spite of herself, it was Amanda's night, Amanda's party.

Fanny came and squeezed her arm. Her eyes were brilliant with a kind of mocking delight, as if to say, "Whatever you're up to, it's fun to watch, you pretty young devil."

Ione stood on her little plump tired feet, smiling and smiling. After a while, Thone edged over. "Sit down, Ione," he said kindly. "Everything's going all right." He drew her to the window seat, sat down beside her himself, and bent toward her to shut away the longing glances of those girls whom he had left twittering uncertainly across the room.

"Seems Amanda's a wow," he said, without expression.

"Yes," said Ione in a rather high voice. In a second she turned to look at him. "Does it annoy you, dear?" He shrugged. "I'm sorry," she said. "Tobias is much too excited. It isn't good for him."

"What can you do?" he murmured.

Her lips turned inward, making her mouth disappear as she bit on them. "Thone, aren't there such things as blood tests? Blood types?"

"Yes."

"Were you ever told? Did they make tests, years ago?"

"Well," he said, crossing a leg, "the thing is, a baby's blood type isn't set for pretty near a year. I suppose such tests might show something. It's all negative, you know. Still they might, for instance, show she could not be the child of my parents. Then again, maybe nothing. If she and I happened to be the same type, d'you see?"

"They never tried that, then?"

"They couldn't, for a year. By that time they didn't think it mattered."

"I suppose it's still possible?"

"To test us now? I'd be glad to have it settled," he said harshly. "I happen to know my type. I'm AB."

"AB," she repeated.

"It's an idea, Ione. We could get Dad's type. But I wonder—if there is a record. Her father is dead, you know. And so is Belle."

"Ah, yes," she said. "It's difficult." She fanned herself with her lacy handkerchief, daintily. Her small feet swung.

"As far as Dad's concerned . . ." Thone turned to look at the room. He saw what was going on. "Oh, God, that picture! Do they always . . . ?"

"Always," said Ione softly, almost plaintively. "They always ask." Her dark eyes seemed to give and expect some sympathy. He sat quite still.

"Belle in the Doorway" hung, now, home from the galleries, on the far wall, hidden by folds of cloth. People were turning to face it. The light above it had gone on. Tobias was about to open the curtains. Ione and Thone, at right angles to their informal ranks, could see, quite plainly, Mandy's profile lifted. The curtains glided with a faint rattling of rings. A solemn hush prevailed in the studio.

Ione's hand came suddenly to Thone's cuff. She was peering. She needn't have nudged him. He was looking at the same thing. At Mandy's face, twisting with her effort not to weep as she gazed, and the tears welling in spite of that in her lovely eyes.

Tobias didn't let them look long. Amanda had turned her back. Fanny had stepped up close to her. Fanny was chattering.

"I suppose," said Ione in a faintly bitter tone, "she has romantic notions about Belle."

"I'm sure of it." Thone let a little contempt into his own voice.

"Has she been told about Belle's death?" Her voice was light, empty. It rode on the surface. Hands played with the handkerchief.

"Oh, yes."

"Who told her?"

"Fanny."

"Oh, Fanny? Oh, dear! Then the poor child's dramatizing, sure enough."

"You bet she is," said he.

"Tragedy," murmured Ione. "Oh, dear!" Her feet swung, alternating. She fanned herself again, beamed brightly at Fanny's face, which turned momentarily toward them from the crowd, as if she knew they'd said her name.

"Thone—" her feet were suddenly still—"do you feel she's like Belle?"

He waited a moment. "Somewhat," he said grudgingly.

She leaned sideways, toward him, as if they swapped gossip behind a fan. "Are you taking your plane tomorrow?"

The stillness of his body was full of caution. His voice said, "I don't think so. This—she makes me fidgety." He didn't meet her eyes.

She put her plump hand on his cuff again. "Don't worry, my dear," said Ione, almost crooning. "It's just a silly romantic girl, walking in a dream."

"I hope she wakes, then," said Thone.

"You don't care for her, do you?" The eyes were shrewd. He shrugged, smiling. "She cares for you, dear."

"I'd rather she didn't," he said. "I hope you're wrong."

Ione said thoughtfully. "These young girls and their notions. You never know how deep it goes, now, do you?"

In her head, scraps of purpose whirled, approached a pattern, and fell away. She was thinking, A girl! A girl is worse than a boy! A million times worse! A boy, a man, who'll go on about his business—that's one thing. But a girl! Here, always, the way she's here now. In that dress. Belle all over again, in a girl's young flesh. Perfumed. . . . Sweet face weeping for Belle! And Toby, talking, talking, talking . . . And she, sitting as Belle used to sit, all ears for him! No!

Thone didn't move. Lace ripped under her fingers. The party foamed around them. He made no sign unless his very immobility had a meaning.

At last he saw, out of the corner of his eye, that the three girls were closing in. He rose. Just then Mandy whirled out of the company, fluid and lovely in the shimmering gown, straight to

Ione. "Is there anything I can do to help?" she begged. "Please let me. I see Elsie is starting. May I help?"

"No, no, my dear. You just be gay." Ione wiggled off the seat, dropped on her two feet, rose.

"Is this your sister?" said the blonde, edging in, drawing the kerchief through her fingers languidly.

"This is Amanda Garth," said Thone flatly. "Whatever is the case, we are most certainly not brother and sister." Amanda's head swung. She was beautiful in surprise.

Ione said, in soft lippety-lippety syllables, "I do think, dear, Amanda's just as glad she cannot be your sister."

Even the shoulders above the ice-green gown seemed to grow rosier in the tide of blood to Mandy's face. She staggered a little, couldn't understand. Her wide eyes went to Ione.

Ione was watching.

The blonde let out a nervous giggle. The brunette shifted her hips contemptuously.

Oh, torn—wide-open! Publicly, in front of these hateful girls! Her heart . . . Amanda rallied. There was nothing to say. She stood quite still. She only knew Ione was watching. She didn't know why. She didn't guess that a little piece of a plan slipped into place. But she felt the malice. It blew on her bare skin. She felt the skin crawl.

She looked up at Thone, forgetting whether she loved him or whether he knew it for sure, now; only wondering if he noticed, too. She thought, with a flicker of fear, that he had noticed.

Ione made a comfortable little purring sound. She tripped

away. Thone bent. "If you're asked, say your blood type is AB," said his quiet voice in her ear.

"Wh-what?"

He didn't repeat. He started to name these girls, to introduce them. Mandy's blood, of whatever type, sang in her veins. He had noticed—noticed something. For now, at last, he conspired!

When the last guest was out the door, Tobias sank down. Ione came behind him to put her firm little paws at his temples, to massage them gently. "Tired, Toby?"

Amanda, sinking in her satin to a chair opposite, watched the hands. Thone was outside, helping unscramble the departing cars.

"Yes, tired," admitted Tobias. "If I had slept . . ." He surrendered to the hands, small strong hands, that stroked and molded.

Amanda met Ione's deep gaze. "Go to bed," it said.

Mandy rose. "I'm tired, too. Do you mind if I go down?"

Tobias smiled. "Don't crush your gown. We must have it tomorrow. You must wear it for your portrait."

"Then she mustn't have tired eyes," said Ione archly. "Come, Amanda, let me make sure there's a light below."

Halfway down the first flight of stairs, Ione said, over her shoulder, "Amanda, do you happen to know—have you ever had your blood typed?"

"Uh-huh. It's AB," said Mandy promptly, beating the jump of her heart. She paused on the step.

Ione drew back as if to let her pass. Her face was calm. "The light is up," she said, nodding dismissal.

"Mrs. Garrison," stammered Mandy, "I can't thank you enough. This is all so exciting and lovely for me. Please," she went on, half artfully, half in confusion, "don't worry over that old baby business. Don't you see? It's too late now. It really doesn't matter any more."

Ione sighed. "You may be right, my dear," she said placidly. "Yes, I do think, after all, that's so. By the way," she added absently, "I put your handkerchief—do you remember?—on your dresser."

"Thank you." Mandy brushed by. "Good night."

"Sleep well." Mandy saved her foot from faltering on the step. She looked back up. Ione leaned there, on the banister.

An echo in Mandy's head said clearly, Peace! The charm's wound up!

12.

Sunday was a weary day. Tobias was haggard. He had not slept for three nights now. Yet, pushed by abnormal energy, he insisted that Mandy pose. So she sat, in light of day and last night's finery. It felt queer. She, too, was tired. She had *not* slept well.

All day there was no signal, no private whisper from Thone. They had no real meeting. She realized that they couldn't have. They must not appear to conspire. But she had to take it on faith that he conspired at all. He was polite to her. Ione could guess whether he were jealous, annoyed, or bored by it all. Guess—but not know.

Tobias could only guess, also. Tobias was aware of his son's aloofness.

Perhaps it was the artist's tension that set them all on edge. Mandy kept suppressing the need to sigh off some of the weight of it. It was a dreadful day!

She thought of Kate, who had, she knew, gone to Catalina with Andrew Callahan and assorted friends. She thought of them in full sunlight, free in the light and the air. For to her, the cool studio was beginning to feel like a corner of hell, in which she was chained by ice-green satin. Also, her heart ached with pity and anxiety for this dear man who worked and talked on, as if unseen devils drove him.

A terrible day!

By nightfall, Tobias was desperately weary. Yet he couldn't rest. And Ione, who had put herself oddly aside all day, moved her hand.

"I do think," she said in her crooning way, "a little of your medicine, Toby, dear. A few nights of rest . . ."

"I suppose so."

"There," she said. "Of course. It will help, dear. It always does." A weary gratitude rolled over the artist's face. He touched her firm little hand and smiled.

"Yes. Please, Ione."

He took the chloral in a glass of milk. No one was anything but casual about it. Ione prepared the dose. The drug was kept, Amanda noticed with surprise, very handy. It was kept on the shelf back of the convenient little serving bar and liquor cabinet in the studio corner.

Had it always been kept there? Oh, but, if so, she thought, then no one but Belle could have touched it six years ago. She thought, I must be all wrong. Ione doesn't like me. But that's all. Nothing's going to happen.

She was not offered anything to drink.

Monday was a little better. They'd shaken down into a routine. Mandy posed in the morning and again in the afternoon. Tobias worked and lectured at the same time. It was very illuminating. Thone answered the phone, ducked invitations. He sun-bathed on the terrace. Or lazed in a fat chair in the studio sometimes, half listening. He was not—not really—interested in painting.

He was a strangely aloof and self-contained creature.

But when he was there, Mandy leaned away to stay upright, as one leans on the west when a west wind is blowing.

Dinner was a peaceful family affair. Thone polite, Ione presiding. Tobias, eating he knew not what, still talking. Tobias took his dose and went early to bed. After he had gone, there seemed to be nothing to talk about.

Nothing happened.

Tuesday morning Thone ambled out to the small breakfast terrace beyond the kitchen, which got almost no eastern sun and was, as Tobias said, one of the stupidities of the house. Nevertheless, Thone wore shorts and a T shirt and was nearly barefoot, with his feet thrust into the cross straps of some very sketchy slippers. He greeted his father, who sat brooding, watching the light change on the hills.

Ione, in crisp blue cotton, came out with her bustling air of keeping this house. Came swiftly, beaming good morning, the glass pot of steaming coffee in her hand. Her neat little feet pattered on the paving stones. She tripped. Perhaps she tripped on a seam. On nothing.

The hot liquid cascaded, all of it, over Thone's bare right foot.

Mandy, coming sleepily up from below the outside way, heard Ione scream, heard Tobias cry out, and Thone's voice bluing the air with blunt language. She ran up the last few steps, braced for catastrophe.

But it was only his foot. A bad burn, to be sure. Ankle, instep, and toes. But only an accident. A stupid, unimportant accident.

"Oh, what a pity!" Ione kept saying. "Oh, poor boy . . ." Tobias went tottering to call a doctor. Burt, the gardener, came to help support Thone's weight and get him into the house. Thone was now silent, very silent. Tense, of course, with the pain.

The doctor came promptly and bound it up, saying comforting words. Not too deep a burn. A matter of days. . . . Thone said little or nothing. The Garrisons did all the talking. They walked at last to the door with the departing doctor.

"Mandy! Come here!"

She went quickly near where he sat in the studio, with his poor foot stiff and helpless.

"Mandy . . ." His fingers went around her wrist. He pulled her close. He was looking up. His face was utterly changed. The mask was gone. An agony in his eyes had nothing to do with physical pain. "Mandy, I'm scared!"

"Why?" she breathed. "Why?"

"When my mother died . . ." She could hardly hear what he was saying. His voice was muted as if his deep alarm robbed it of strength. "I had a bad foot."

"Oh," she gasped. She bent down. Her lips near his hair.

"Mandy, for God's sake, will you stay with me?"

"Yes . . . yes."

"If it's a pattern?" he said, "I don't think she—tripped." He kept his hand tight on her wrist but he closed his eyes, and when he opened them they were less wild. "It could be suggestion," he admitted.

"I know," she agreed quickly. "The whole thing. We've rigged it against her. She can't help but hate me. I know that. Anyone would."

He moved his fingers and now her whole hand was warm inside his. "Did she ask about your blood?"

She nodded. "I said what you told me."

"Same as mine. Just to confuse," he explained. "Oh, Lord, I was scared there for a minute."

"Does it hurt?" she whimpered.

"Like hell." He smiled fleetingly. "But it isn't that." He looked behind them and again the color and strength went out of his voice. "I can barely hobble. It's the same as it was before." And he shuddered. His wide shoulders shook.

Mandy said blindly, "Oh, maybe not, maybe not. Maybe she didn't . . ." She could feel, as if it were in her own heart, his shuddering horror. Ah, if Belle, so beloved, had been *sent* away! If, these six years, her lost radiance was less lost than stolen! She put her mouth against his hair. It was impossible not to. Impossible.

His head, tilting, brushed her lips. "Mandy, will you go find a man named Kelly? El Kelly, they call him. Pasadena police. Your eyes are fresh. See what there was when my mother died. If I could, I'd go and do that now myself. Will you do it, Mandy?"

"Of course," she said. "Today."

"Come up the outside way tonight. My little balcony." He looked behind again.

"We'll have to make sure," she said quietly. "Now you can't bear not to know for sure. Now it has seemed possible . . . I understand."

He let go her hand, a gentle releasing. "You're the only one," he said, as if he apologized for troubling her.

She walked away a little. A deep trembling seemed to be shaking her whole body, although she walked steadily enough. It didn't enter her mind, then—not then—that any pattern that might be forming had herself for its center. She thought it was terrible for him if it was true. Terrible for him even to have to wonder. Yet she was shaking with guilty joy.

For she would stay with him. She would be with him. She was the only one he could turn to, the way things had fallen.

13.

Tobias had been too much upset by the accident to work that morning. Ione ministered to him, as well as to Thone. She was the woman of the house, in control, firm and cheerful. She coaxed at their spirits, she brought tidbits and pillows, she was serene and busy. They must lean on her strength. All would be well. She was the captain. The ship of the house sailed on.

Lunch was served in the studio for Thone's sake. He seemed half drowsy with the codeine he'd been given, but out of pain and perfectly calm.

Amanda chose a moment at the end of lunch to exclaim, "Golly!" Everyone looked at her. "I forgot! Oh, golly! I'll have to go up to school. I never did sign my schedule."

"Will it be open?" asked Thone sleepily.

"The office will be. Maybe this afternoon would be a good time." She turned to the artist. "Or will you want to work, sir?"

"I doubt it, Mandy." His smile was all affection.

"He should not work," said Ione. "So you run along, my dear. Would you like to take my car?"

Mandy's lips opened. It could pass for awed delight.

"Can you manage it?" said Ione. "I'm sure you can, you California child. I shan't use it today." She looked smug, as if she congratulated herself upon her devotion to the stricken house. "By all means . . ."

"If you really don't mind . . ." said Amanda slowly.

"My dear, I shouldn't offer if I minded." Ione was Mrs. Santa Claus, pleased to please. She nodded and twinkled.

"Such a beautiful car! Thank you, Mrs. Garrison."

"I'll fetch you the keys," Ione went trotting.

Thone sat very still. Even counting the calming dose he'd been given, it was too still. Mandy found herself stiffening into the same kind of quiet. Tobias was finishing his cake. "My dear," he said with normal fussy affection, "you'll be careful, won't you?" He wiped his lips.

"I'll be careful," said Mandy.

Ione brought a small leather case in which hung a great many keys. She opened the zipper and selected two. "This is for the garden door. You just walk in, going down, but when you come back you'll need it. So I've tied a bit of string on it. There. This is the ignition. Better hold it, dear. It'll save fumbling. Now, can you find your way? Do you know what to do? The middle door's not locked. You just go through. The garage doors have a bar inside. Just lift it and slam them open. Do you understand?" She purred these instructions.

Mandy said, "I know the way."

"Just leave the big doors open. The garden door protects us. Will you be long, my dear?"

"Not long, I guess," said Mandy vaguely. "I'll be back for dinner, of course."

"Good," said Ione cheerily.

Holding the right key in her fingers, Mandy went down through the house, snatched her purse and her short coat from her room, and went out through the lower door. She started down the paths, the turns and twists, the steps, the whole rambling, zigzagging descent into the canyon. She moved along the slope. Halfway down, she knew she went in terror.

Down to the place of death.

A shrine, he'd called it. Oh, God, prayed Mandy, let me remember that. Let me not begin to wonder, now, just how she did it. Or how Belle went down in the dark, this way, and died on the floor. Or how that little creature managed to make it happen. Let me not think about those things.

She moved along rather slowly, but steadily. She came to the workshop door, what Ione had called the garden door. The knob rattled in her nervous hand. The door was quite thick and sturdy. Worked by some sort of spring, it closed slowly and with ponderous finality, by itself, behind her. Closed and locked, she realized. She stood there a moment, in the queer light that came uncannily through the glass bricks in the wall. Bracing herself for the place, the garage, that box, so stuffed and filled with the big car, so small and closed in, so cavelike . . . Would there be air? Could she breathe in there?

She threw back her shoulders, marched the little way to the middle door, and tugged it open.

So dim, down there. She tasted something bitter in her mouth. The taste of fear. She ran. Knowing that the door she released was moving behind her to close her in, she ran down the steps, past the shining body of the car, and almost in a panic bore her strength upward on the bar. The doors creaked and parted. It was all right.

She could breathe.

Sweat beading her face, Mandy pushed them wide. She leaned on each door then, pressing it back firmly into the grasp of its retaining hook. She shook each door a little. Both seemed to hold. She arranged the ignition key, ready, in her hand. She went swiftly to the car, got in, started the motor with the muscles of her leg sending long tremors up her body. She backed out, fast. The car popped forth.

She was free. She was under the sky.

Mandy drew a long shuddering breath and felt a little ashamed. She pushed back her hair. She drove out the lower road and felt the sun on her face.

Ellis Kelly, called El, so that he sounded like a Hibernian relic of old Spanish days, was a hard-faced man of about forty-five. His lair was not hard to come upon. Fortunately, he was in it. When, after half an hour of waiting, Mandy was admitted to his presence, he met her with a cold, professionally suspicious stare.

But Amanda was not going to be daunted. She chose to be both crisp and appealing. "Lieutenant Kelly, six years ago you were in charge or at least involved in the investigation of the accidental death of Mrs. Belle Garrison."

"I was."

"I've come because her son, Thone Garrison, asked me to come and talk to you."

"Yeah?"

"My name is Amanda Garth. I'm a guest at their house."

"Yeah?"

"Was there anything about that accident—" now she was a little less crisp and a little more appealing—"that makes you wonder?" she finished.

"You got a suspect?" he said coldly, so quickly it was as if she'd put her fingers near a trap and been caught.

"I might have," she said.

"Who?"

She caught her lip in her teeth. He simply waited, turning a pencil between his hands. "Mrs. Tobias Garrison," said Mandy boldly. "Ione, his first wife. Now she's his wife again. The one who died was—in between."

"Uh-huh," he said. "What do you know?"

"I don't know a darned thing," cried Mandy in exasperation. "I came to ask *you.*"

"You got a feeling?" said El Kelly. "Or is it this son who's got a feeling?"

"Both of us."

"Uh-huh," he said. "Well, Miss Garth. Feelings have causes. They don't come from nowhere. Whether the feeling you've got is caused by something inside or outside . . ." He lowered his head. He looked up at her from under his brows.

"We don't *know* whether it's just in our heads, or whether it comes from her," said Mandy. "That's exactly why I've come here."

He got up and went to some files. In no time at all he had extracted a sheaf of papers. "We'll take a look," he said.

Mandy breathed deeply. She smiled at him.

"What was it that's bothering you?"

She found it difficult to say. At last she told him, picking her words carefully to be clear, about the sleeping potion in the chocolate. She did not tell him how she came to be there. Nor did she mention the confusion about her birth. She did not say how she felt. It made a bald little tale. Poison, how she knew. Gene. The handkerchief destroyed.

He listened. "You figure she changed her mind?"

"Yes."

"A tough thing for me to do anything about," he told her. "Depends on what you and this chemist say. Nothing else to show. Nobody got hurt."

"I know."

"You figure that if she's up to something now, maybe she was up to something then, six years ago?"

"Oh, yes," said Mandy gratefully. "That's it."

He glanced at the papers he held and sighed. "I'll tell you frankly, Miss Garth, I'm never satisfied with anything so screwy as this accident. But I've got to have evidence, and I never had any. Since you bring it up, I remember Mrs. Ione. Struck me, right away, she'd have a motive. I went so far as to see did she have an alibi that night."

"Did she?"

"Nothing much good. But that's convincing, in a way. Lived alone. So who's always got an alibi?" He shrugged. "Trouble is, if she had anything to do with it, how? She wasn't there."

"That's what they say."

"No trace of her."

"N-none?"

"Take a look." He shoved the papers across the desk.

Mandy said, "Thank you." She began to look at them. They were typed reports of interviews, for the most part. Doctor . . . Tobias . . . Elsie . . . Burt . . . William Cheeseman, Consolidated cab . . .

That would be Belle's cab driver. She began to read a part of it.

A: I got a call at nine-twenty. I was up there looking for the place about ten or fifteen minutes later. She was waiting outside the gate. She gives me a hail.

Q: What did she say?

A: She says, "Hey, cab. You, green cab." So I stop. She says, "Are you for Mrs. Garrison?" I says, "Yes." She says, "I've changed my mind. It's so far I think I'd rather drive myself. Here's for your trouble." So she hands me a couple of bucks. Two dollars, that is. And she says, "You can go up this way and get down the other side of the canyon." So I says, "O.K., lady, suit yourself."

Q: Was the light good? Could you see her?

A: Sure. Sure I could see her. She had a blue scarf tied over her head, kinda tied under her chin. Had a dark coat. She had some keys in her hand.

Q: You recognized her, then?

A: Sure. Sure, it was Mrs. Garrison, all right.

Q: You knew the lady?

A: Sure. Poor lady. Looking back now, I remember she acted kind of funny.

Q: You noticed that she was under the influence of a drug?

A: Maybe that was it.

Mandy turned the paper over. Thone's statement.

Q: Age?

A: Seventeen.

Q: Deceased was your mother?

A: Yes, sir.

Mandy skipped down the page.

A: . . . Dad went to the phone. Somebody had a little painting of his he'd lost. He was crazy to get it back, naturally.

Oh, Thone, wept Mandy. "Naturally". . . not blaming Dad.

Q: She intended to take a cab, didn't she?

A: Yes, sir. She asked me to call one for her.

Q: You were laid up with that foot?

A: Yes, sir. I couldn't walk easily. But we have a long cord on our phone. Mother brought me the phone. She went to her room to get ready. I called a couple of places. Finally I got one. She came back, all ready to go. . . . We didn't go to the door with her. Dad had a cold.

Oh, Thone, wept Mandy.

Q: She said nothing about driving herself?

A: No, sir. We can't understand it.

Mandy turned the page. Burt Gibbons, gardener.

Q: The extra keys to the garage and the car were kept in a drawer in the hall?

A: Yes, sir. Always. I'd be the only one would use them once in a while.

Q: When did you see them last?

A: About a week or so ago.

Q: Mrs. Garrison knew they were there?

A: Oh, yes, sir.

Mandy shook her head. Tobias, his statement.

Q: You didn't touch the chloral, the box with the powders in it, yourself at all?

A: No. No one did. Except my wife.

Elsie Gibbons, cook-housekeeper.

Q: You washed up the glasses that had been used?

A: Yes, sir. I always do. Can't leave them set overnight.

Q: You ever touch the box of medicine?

A: No, sir, never. Mrs. Garrison took care of that herself.

El Kelly said, rumbling, "Screwy thing. *Two* accidents, you'd say. First, she gets a knockout dose. Then, it has to hit her just exactly on the wrong minute. After the engine is started. But before the doors are fastened wide-open. Quite a coincidence, eh?"

"Ye-es," said Mandy. "It was." She riffled the papers. No statement from Ione was there.

"That's why it passed through my mind," Kelly said, "it could be suicide."

"Suicide! Belle!"

"Well, take a look. She gets those keys, says nothing to her family, does she? She sends the cab away. Funny, if she almost never drives herself, as they say. Certainly looks like she must have handled the chloral. All right. Why couldn't it be that she goes down there, starts the engine, fixes the doors to look right, lies down on the floor, right under the exhaust . . ."

"But why?"

"Why'd she try to make it look like an accident? For the kid's sake, maybe."

"Oh!" Mandy sat back, tingling with alarm. "But why?" she cried again. "Why would she do that? For what reason?"

"I don't know," he said. "But I've got a hunch the old gentleman agrees with me."

"Tobias!"

"Yeah. Maybe *he* knows a reason. He'd keep it from the kid, too, you know."

She thought, Is this why Tobias doesn't face it? Is this his sorrow? Is this what hurts him so? That Belle wanted to die . . . She put her face in her hands.

El Kelly gathered up the papers and straightened them. "You can look at it a lot of ways," he said. "You're kinda friendly with the son," he went on calmly. "Reason I say all this to you . . . maybe it isn't such a good idea for him to start figuring out what really happened. Get what I mean?"

"Yes, I do," said Mandy shakily. "I—thank you very much."

"Don't like to see people feeling any worse than they need to feel," he said, still hard-faced and stern. "I'd call the truth, if I was sure what it was. But . . ." He shrugged his shoulders. "Get what I mean?"

Oh, what have I done! cried Mandy to herself. Oh, what have I done!

14.

Afternoon shadows filled the bowl of the canyon early, and deepened, flooding upward to engulf the lower part of the house first and then rise, story by story, until by five o'clock only the topmost floor caught a little last sunlight, although on the other rim of the canyon and on the mountaintops the land was yet warm and bright.

Mandy crept in at the lowest point of the house. Her room was dim and chilly. She washed, she fixed her face. She felt numb and calm. The energy of fear had left her. She felt that she had been meddling feverishly and ignorantly, indeed, and now the consequences would have to be met. Somehow, she would have to endure the rest of this week-long visit, endure Thone's stirred-up agonies of doubt, hold herself steady, and without giving anything away, let emotions storm about her and fall of their own falseness to nothing.

She went up through the house. Thone's door was closed. She could hear voices behind it. Feeling outcast, accepting the feeling, she went by.

Up in the studio, Ione sat alone. "Oh, Amanda. How is my car?" She amended this quickly. "Did it behave?"

"It behaved beautifully." Mandy gave her the keys. Ione's hand closed greedily over the key case. It was plain that she hadn't liked lending her car. Her car . . . her own . . . It crossed Amanda's mind to wonder why, then, she had been so obliging. But the thought was fleeting.

On the round table, between two fat chairs, were tall glasses. Ione herself had been sipping something. "Sit down, Amanda." She put a finger on the tabletop and turned it a quarter of a circle. The used glasses moved as the tabletop revolved. "Fanny's here. Thone was worn out and we felt he should be in bed. Burt helped him down. Now Toby's taken Fanny to see him. We've had a wee nip. My dear, you do look tired. You must have something, too."

She wiggled forward to bring her dangling little feet to the floor. She rose. "I'm afraid Thone's accident upset you."

"I guess it did." Amanda let her head fall against the chair. She looked up passively, contritely. "I wonder if I'd better stay," she said, eyes smoky with self-blame.

Something stiffened on the jolly round-cheeked little face. "Now, now," chided Ione, "of course you'll stay." She pattered the length of the room to the bar in the corner. "Come here, my dear." Mandy got up obediently and walked after her. "See what there is here that strikes your fancy." Ione's voice was chipper and a little false, as if she poked up a mood of gaiety. "Something to cheer you up a little."

To cheer me up, thought Mandy. She felt on her head the coals of fire. She was seeing Ione from another angle, as if she were perfectly innocent. If it were so, Amanda was ashamed.

Ione held open the doors of the liquor cabinet, revealing bottles. "I don't much care about drinking . . ." Amanda began. She was offering, in some way, her apologies. She was feeling there was much to be paid for, wrong done that must be undone. And since it had never been directly stated to this woman's face, it could not be denied, except in an attitude, an inner difference.

The little brisk right hand darted among the bottles and pulled one forth. One certain bottle. "Some of this, perhaps?" she asked brightly.

Amanda read the label. "Legendre . . . Herbsaint . . ." Her skin pricked. Her face, she knew, was giving away her recognition. This was Belle's drink. The very stuff! The drink she'd been so fond of—Belle's firewater! Her breath drew in, making a sound. Dark eyes were on her. Ione knew what she offered. She had a purpose.

Why? Why? What was the purpose? The whole structure of apology collapsed in Mandy's mind. Wild speculations rushed in and filled its place. Could this be the very bottle? Was chloral in there? Now? Still? Was it possible? Had the bottle itself been doped? Was that how Belle got it?

Oh, no, no, no. Impossible! Surely El Kelly would have checked such a simple, obvious thought. It could not be that Ione was offering, here, now, after six years, a dose of chloral! Giving the trick away! Or didn't she know? Was it an innocent choice?

No, not innocent, no accident. She offered Herbsaint and she watched. But why did she offer it and what was she watching for? What was in her mind? What was she up to? Mandy braced herself. Whatever it meant, she knew she must play out the part, all the way. Belle's favorite, was it? Very well.

"That I love!" said Mandy boldly. "That I adore!"

"Then you shall have some." The white head seemed to tremble, as if it wanted to nod, "I thought so," and was trying not to nod. The face twinkled. The hands were brisk, quick, unhesitating. "And there you are!" said Ione, almost triumphantly.

Amanda went back and sat down. She sipped. It was firewater, all right. She struggled not to gasp and choke. It was horrid, she thought. Resolutely she sipped it. Eyes staring ahead, she seemed to be dreaming, brooding. . . . Ione was quiet as a mouse. She was picking at the bit of string on the workshop key.

Amanda thought, If there is any of that stuff in here, I shall pass out, presently. She followed the burning warmth down her throat, down to where it might slowly, mysteriously enter her blood, rise to her brain, perhaps . . . touch, alter, destroy the conscious self. She thought, how frail we are in our ignorance! What potions there are in the world whose magic we so little understand!

Ione thought, It's true, after all. She does dramatize. Look at her, look at her now. So it will be quite plausible, when she follows Belle.

Fanny came up alone. "Ah, there you are, my dearie! Hi, Amanda Garth. How is it going?"

"F-fine," said Amanda. She got up, wondering if she'd fall.

Fanny's quick eye took in the tiny glass in her hand. "What's that you're drinking?"

"Herbsaint," said Amanda, stammering.

"God's grief!" said Fanny softly. The bright friendship in her face went glimmering. Cold disappointment took its place. The change of her expression was as sharp as a slap. Amanda staggered.

"Cab's coming," said Fanny. "Good-by, Ione." She put her arm affectionately across that little lady's shoulder. They moved off toward the hall. Mandy, abandoned, stared after them. Fanny turned her head and-looked-baek—as if it were the prick of her manners that made her fling it over her shoulder. "Oh, good-by."

"Ione, why don't you kick her out!" In the hall, Fanny took her arm away.

Ione said softly, "Oh, now, Fan. She's thinking of herself all glamorous, like poor dead Belle."

"I would kick her out," said Fanny viciously, "for just that reason. By the way, I'm coming to dinner Thursday. They said to ask you. I'm telling you, of course."

"Thursday?" said Ione doubtfully.

"Cook's night out. I would. But it's all I've got. Potluck, Ione. You won't mind me. I won't make any difference."

"I won't mind, of course not," said Ione pleasantly. "You won't make any difference, Fanny. On the contrary," she twinkled archly, "perhaps you'll help."

"Not with the dishes. Don't bank on that." Fanny pinched her and grinned and went away.

Ione stood, hands lightly clasped, and over her lip she slowly ran her tongue. She hadn't been thinking of the dishes.

15.

It was very quiet in the canyon at night. Few cars ran on the mountain roads. Only now and then someone who lived in the hills came home, or a guest departed. There was no real traffic. No street noises. No pedestrians, naturally. The hills slept. Birds called intermittently. Sometimes, in the wild dry chaparral that coated all slopes not cleared and kept clear by a man, there was a rustle of small wild life, going about its ancient business, near the ground.

Moonlight touched the high places, but not this part of the slope, west of the house, where Mandy was climbing, soft as an animal herself in the dark. Barefoot, because she had brought no rubber soles, she felt carefully for each step, keeping her finger tips lightly on the wall, crouching past Burt's and Elsie's window, going up.

Thone's west window had a little railed platform outside. Underneath the ground pitched. If she climbed far enough, the inner edge of the balcony would be only shoulder high. Her hands were on the white-painted bars. She found a firm spot for her feet.

"Mandy." He was there. It was so small a balcony that only

part of his body was out the window. He half lay on the floor. His cheek was flat on the wood. His breath was on her forehead. His whisper was not even sibilant. It was so nearly not a sound at all she might almost have heard him think her name.

"Thone?" She tried to swallow sound, as he did. She brought her head a little higher, rested her cheek on a bar. "I don't think we'll be heard," he said. "She has no windows on this side."

"I was quiet. No one heard me."

"Burt's a little deaf."

She clung there silently a moment. They listened to the night.

"What about Kelly? Did you . . . ?"

"I saw him," she said. "There was nothing."

"Nothing?"

"No." The cold bar felt strong. The edge of it cut her face with welcome pain. "He was very nice. But there was nothing."

"I made Burt find my crutch," he said irrelevantly. "It was still in the storeroom."

"Is the pain bad?"

"No, no, not now. Unless I put my weight on it."

"Thone, what does Fanny think?"

"I told her you had a delusion. I told her I thought it was wise to have you up here; said I was afraid of what you'd do. But Fanny's all for you."

Not any more, she thought.

"What is it, Mandy? Are you frightened?"

"No."

"There's something exhausted about you. What's the matter?"

"I'm all right."

He moved his head. "You've had something to drink."

"Just a liqueur." She felt helpless. No use. He'd caught it on her breath. He would have to be told about it, right away.

"When?" he asked.

"Once, before dinner. After dinner she offered me some more."

"*She* did?"

"It's been hours," said Mandy defensively. "I haven't passed out. Nothing happened." She knew that if he hadn't felt he must be quiet, he'd have said something sharp and probably profane. "It was Herbsaint," she confessed. "I thought I'd better be fond of it."

It took him a while before he answered. He said slowly, "Something's cooking, all right."

"Yes," she said simply.

"Sure as hell, something. Mandy, I'm convinced. There is too much, too much like it was before. Dad's taking chloral. As he was then. I've got a bum foot. Now you're drinking Herbsaint after dinner. Do you notice—every one of those three facts started with Ione?"

"Not your father's chloral."

"She suggested it. You heard her. He used to fight it a lot longer. Mandy, I *know.*"

"Oh."

"Pattern," he said. "Maybe it's not so plain to you. But I was here."

"It's pretty plain," she said.

He moved, it seemed, closer. "Has it occurred to you, you've done what you set out to do?"

"What do you mean?"

"You've got me believing, and I'm watching out. I'm on my guard. Now, go home."

"Go home?"

"Yes. You go home."

"But—"

"Tonight. Or early tomorrow," he insisted.

She said, "Wouldn't that bust up the pattern?"

"Yes."

Mandy said, "No."

"For God's sake, you don't think I'm really going to pull up a chair and watch you—get hurt!"

"Oh, no, not really, but—"

"There's no 'but.' I believe you, even about the damn poison. So now you get out of here."

"But if I do—"

"I can convince her there's nothing in this baby mixing. You know damn well I can. So could you, if you tried. You'll be right out of it. We've got as far as we can get with that foolishness."

"Wait," said Mandy. "What is it? What is the pattern?"

"The pattern of my mother's death," he said.

"You mean, for me?"

"For you."

"Maybe we're wrong. Maybe . . ."

He read her mind. What she couldn't phrase, he got without phrases. "Let me tell you something. If she's repeating that pattern, she's not copying *nature*."

"That's what I wondered," she said gratefully.

"No, it means there was a pattern then, too. It wouldn't drift into her head, that design, unless she'd done some work on it before. I'm *sure* of that."

Her fingers ached on the bars. She agreed, deeply. She was sure of it, too. "But then," she said, "we'll have to know the whole pattern."

"What?"

"We don't know how she did it before."

"No."

"But if this is the same pattern over again, why, she's going to show us how she did it. Isn't she? All we have to do is watch her."

"Not if it's you," he said in a kind of horror.

"It's too late," said Mandy, "to change that part of it. The way it's working out, it has to be me."

"I won't have—"

"Ssh."

He squirmed in the dark. "It's my risk. I won't have you or anybody else taking it."

"But I've got it!" said Mandy. Her heart lightened. "I don't intend to die," she said almost gaily.

"I don't intend to let you come even close." His whisper was fierce. She felt happy. "Your mother would skin me alive," he added.

"Then she'd better not know a thing about it," said Mandy rather testily. "But we are watching, we are aware. And Ione doesn't have any idea that we are. You'll be outside the—plot. You can step in and stop it in time."

"Too dangerous," he muttered.

"It's not so very, as long as you're looking out for me."

"My God!" said Thone. He rolled on his back.

She squirmed even nearer, shifting her cramped bare toes.

"You know something's cooking. And so do I. Well, that's good! It's giving us a chance. It's the only kind of chance we *could* have against her. What else can you do, Thone? If you send me away, then you'll have to wait until she starts a new plan. Against you, maybe. You'd be all alone—nobody to help, the way I have you." She hurried on. "And suppose it didn't follow the pattern? Even if you caught her at it, how could you prove anything about six years ago? Or suppose she just never tried anything again? Then you'd think all your life about her and Belle. Don't you see? Now, there's me, and I fit right into the same pattern. So let her keep going. You'll be ready. Nothing will happen to me. And you'll know. You'll *know*."

She thought to herself, And Tobias will know! That Belle never wanted to leave him at all. There's some good in that. Anyhow, he can't be left living with a murderer. She said, "Oh, please, Thone. Do it this way? I'm not afraid!"

"Yes, you are," he said flatly.

"Well, what of it?" she defied.

"*I'm* afraid," he said, "God knows."

"What about the—pattern? What else do you think?"

"Probably her car. You've taken it out yourself once now. You know the way down. Maybe that fits, too."

"Yes," she agreed. "I'll be asked to drive it again, you think?"

"Maybe."

"Because you wouldn't drive, with your foot. No one would ask you to. Your father wouldn't be asked, either."

"Burt will have to be out, though. He was out before. It was a Thursday."

The night breeze was chilly.

"Then, Thursday?" she breathed.

"Thursday."

The iron bar was cold on her face. She moved her cheek against it. "But how *can* she . . . ?"

"We don't know how."

"That's what we'll have to know. Thone, it's too close. Thursday! We can't give up!"

"You can."

"No."

She felt him move restlessly in the dark. "Mandy, why do you want to do this? Is it because you think you're in love with me?" All nuance of feeling was lost in the flat muted whisper.

"Certainly, I am in love with you," she said in the same way. "I know how *you* feel. It's O.K. It has nothing to do with it." He was still.

"Listen," she said. "You've got to know how your mother died. I've got to help you find out, because I started the whole business, kind of. That's all. That's the only way you and I are together. I know that."

He made no answer.

"If I were a male, you'd be tickled to death," she accused. "Your pal, I'd be. You'd think it was all right to let me take a chance. You'd grant that." He stirred, but didn't speak. "All right," she went on, "let me make it perfectly clear. I'd be awfully pleased, naturally, if you should fall in love with me. But I realize probably you aren't going to, and I can take it if you don't. And we'll cross that bridge when we come to it, anyhow."

"God damn it!" he said aloud. Then whispered, angrily, "What do you think I'm afraid of?"

"Oh, being hurt again," she said bluntly. "By a dumb loving female." She clung there. She smiled in the dark.

He lay flat on his back. He started to say, "Fanny talks too much." Then he said no more. The night sky wheeled over their heads. Small creatures stirred. A eucalyptus tree bent its tall ragged head in a passing current of air. She could feel the paralyzed knot in his throat. Maybe it was cruel to keep quiet.

"My feet hurt," said Mandy suddenly. "I haven't got any shoes on. Please say we'll go ahead on a common-sense basis."

He said, "You win," in a queer choked way. She took one hand off the bar, reached in, and patted blindly. She hit him half in the eye. His fingers caught hers. "I swear to God," he whispered, "I don't know what else to do, you being the character you are."

"That's fine." She ripped her hand away. She was afraid he'd hear the tear that was slipping out of her eye. She let herself down.

Thone lay on his back in the dark. All her cautious way down, she knew he was lying there. She thought, Well, anyhow, I was honest! She thought, So my pride was hanging around my heels in rags and tatters, anyway. She thought, Well, anyhow, it's got to be this way. I had to hit him over the head with it. I can't go home. She thought, But I hope it's over quickly. I hope to goodness it's *this* Thursday I'm supposed to die! She thought, But that's ridiculous! Die?

Her body was lithe and moved, alive, in the dark. Her breath used the air. Her cold toes felt of the earth. Her hand, that marvelous thing, a living hand, was sentient on the wall.

16.

In the morning, at the breakfast table, Ione said, "Toby, I've called the repair man to come fetch your car. It needs going over. It'll only be a day or two, he says. Perhaps by Friday or Saturday . . . You'll want to be with Thone, of course, just now, and there's always mine."

"Of course, my dear," said Tobias mildly.

Of course, thought Mandy, of course. It clicked right down. It fitted in snugly. There is always my car! Ah, but what she meant to say was, There will be only mine. As before. As there had been only one car available to the household six years ago, and it down in the canyon!

"Do you take sugar, Mandy?" she heard Thone say politely.

"Yes, I do. Thank you." The turn of her head was miraculously gracious and controlled.

"Shall we work today?" asked Tobias, "or are you too tired, child? I'm afraid I'm spoiling your visit."

"Since she is getting roughly the equivalent of a four-year course for free," drawled Thone, "I don't think she's complaining."

Amanda swallowed hard. "Heavens, of course I'm not complaining!" She put her chin up, smiled at Tobias. Her thoughts were on this pattern of their own. She knew Thone was right to be cool or worse to her. She felt that Ione had noticed and would notice everything between them. Indeed, everything between Amanda and anyone. So she smiled, radiantly, at Tobias. But she didn't see him. She wasn't looking for the subtle reaction on the father's face. She forgot, and Thone forgot, that Tobias was also a receiving instrument.

They played for Ione. Tobias, also, saw the show.

It was decided to get on with the portrait.

Ice-green satin! She could have ripped it off her shoulders and thrown it down and trampled on it. Someday she would. But for now she had to sit still, with her spine straight and yet easy, with her face turned to the light, with her hands quiet.

Thone, using his crutch, got nimbly to the sofa. She could not even look in his direction. He had to sit there with his foot up and pretend to drowse or read, while Wednesday went by. While Tobias worked along. While Ione kept the house. . . .

Mandy began to think about Belle, Belle in all her pretty costumes. What was the rose-and-gold ball gown made of? she wondered. Satin? "And a golden rose for her hair." What had she worn to die? Mandy wrenched her mind from that. What had she worn on the islands? Something gay, no doubt. Color, of course. Coral, bright pinks, hibiscus shades. Thone would remember her in luscious color. His whole boyhood must have been soaked in brilliance and laughter. Mandy knew, because it was there in those paintings, in the laughing quality of the island paintings. That deep, bright happiness! She wondered dreamily how Thone could escape wanting to paint. Why was he, in a way, so somber, with his feeling for form, shape, mass, line. Had Belle been so? She puzzled and dreamed, forgetting. . . .

Tobias worked along. He was saying very little. He was working slowly. The first quick, sure, eager, plunging certainty of this work was over. The thrill was gone. He had not worked like that for years now. He would never reach it again, never touch it, the magic.

What had excited him so, if it had not been a brief revival of old magic? Now he felt heavy. He felt old again. Oh, he was skilled and disciplined. His hand would not fail. He would command it delicately and it would obey. An obedient hand! Ah, not the same thing as body and soul that flowed, all one substance, out at the finger tips!

He would teach this sweet girl all he knew, and it would amount to very little, after all. For who could teach magic? It was given, it arrived. . . . And when it was gone, one called for it in vain.

He was old, but not dull enough. Things hit on his naked nerve ends. He was battered and tossed. He was defenseless against so many intangible buffets. Thone, so remote and tense, so cautious and closed up against contact . . . Pale marks on this girl's cheeks, barely preceptible new planes in this young face . . . Spiritual breezes that blew from he knew not what source, in which he swayed and staggered as they passed him by.

He was not strong any more. Not able to understand, not told, and yet, pitifully, not indifferent, either.

They were so young. He wished . . . He wished . . . In their new and complicated world, which they must understand, if he did not, he wished they were standing together. But he feared . . . he felt . . .

He did not know why he began to cry in his heart, to hunt back down the years for her. For Belle.

Ione had a letter in the afternoon mail.

> About the fuchsias [it ran], if you insist, my dear, of course. Although it's a hell of a way from where you are to the airport. Our flight leaves, as I think I told you, at ten-five P.M. I'd run them out to you, gladly, but I'm crazy with packing, you can imagine. However, I could easily do it in a week or so, after we've come home. So for pity's sake, if you can't get down there Thursday, don't worry. I'll stick the cuttings in the checkroom with your name on them, and remember, if they die, we can always take more.

Ione folded the sheet of pale blue paper over the backhanded scrawl. "Barbara McPhail! Why, the dear girl!" she exclaimed, her eyes round with pleasure. "Toby, what do you think! She's going to give me a mess of green cuttings from her wonderful fuchsias!"

"Very nice," said Tobias, squinting at his palette.

"She and Charles are flying to Seattle tomorrow. She'll bring them as far as the airport. Isn't that dear of her?"

Thone's sleepy lids lifted.

"I shall have to just run down," said Ione. "I hope Burt and I can root them. She has such a clever man who comes in once a week. He'll pack them moist, I hope."

"Airport?" said Thone. His voice was almost empty of significance, barely even curious. Mandy's fingers in her lap curled suddenly.

"Inglewood. Oh, dear, it is a drive," Ione lamented. "Let's see, if their plane goes at ten, they'll plan to be there in good time—by nine-thirty, I should think."

"How long will they be in Seattle?" asked Tobias absently.

"My dear, she doesn't say," lied Ione. "It's so sweet of her to think of me before they go away. I must tell Burt."

"Burt can fetch them," murmured Tobias. Ione didn't answer. She didn't remind him that tomorrow night Burt would be out. She went trotting on her little feet as if to arrange, to see about it, to give her happy orders.

"Lovely things, fuchsias," said Tobias. "Barbara's, especially."

On the girl's face, in the light, there was a strange tightening of the skin on the bones, as if the softly rounded young flesh were thinning and failing before his eyes.

"God damn this foot!" Thone's sudden violence was a shock. "Excuse me, Dad—Amanda." Amanda caught her breath. The shock shook and relaxed her.

Tobias put his brush down and looked curiously at his hand. "We'll stop. Amanda is tired and so am I. And Thone is bored." He hoped it was so. He looked at their faces pleadingly. At their suddenly bland young faces, their blank, though smiling, eyes.

Not once did Ione leave the house that day. That Wednesday. Burt ran the errands. The day dragged on as if Time itself had open jaws and they were narrowing, slowly, slowly, as the clock ticked.

After dinner Tobias had his dose, reached for it eagerly, for the sleep it promised, for some integrating rest, however found. Amanda had her Herbsaint. It was already the tradition of the house. It was a matter of course.

Thone said in that lazy voice, so emptied of meaning, "I say, Ione, how about me?"

"Whisky, dear?"

"No, I think I'll try the same." He stretched and grinned, playing bored.

"Ah, but I shall have whisky," trilled Ione. "Amanda, dear, will you come, take these?"

So Amanda went to fetch the pretty little glasses, the dainty stemmed glasses from the bar. "I think I was stingy," said Ione sharply. So Amanda smiled and touched the bottle that looked so much like a wine bottle but that held Belle's firewater. She put a little more Herbsaint in each glass. Ione's hands were both busy. Jigger in one, ice tongs in the other. "Look out for the . . ." She pointed with her elbow. Amanda's hand touched the box that held the chloral.

"This?"

"Thanks, dear. Just push it away from the edge—there."

I am very obliging, thought Amanda. Very obliging am I. If she wanted me to touch it, now I've touched it. I shall do everything she seems to suggest, quite willingly. Although I will be taking notes. I must go along with her . . . to a point, to a point. It must run smoothly, as far as she knows. And how smoothly it does go! How easy it must seem! Nothing has happened at all. And yet so much. All bits and pieces, each so innocent. Bits and pieces of a pattern. So we really see a pattern? Are the jaws of Wednesday closing down? Will it be Thursday, tomorrow?

She felt strange, as if she were drifting. She brought Thone his glass. "Nice night out," he muttered, with a dark restless look.

"Poor Thone, poor boy," crooned Ione. "So uncomfortable. So confined. Never mind. It'll soon be healed. I'm so glad it's no worse." She sighed. She beamed around her, at the family, the cozy end of Wednesday.

17.

Not quite ended.

It *was* a nice night out. But Amanda knew he'd meant her to come. So she climbed, in the dark, with the most delicate care. He was waiting for her, sprawled on the balcony floor. Lips at her ear, he said, "It's plain, isn't it? You'll be the one to go for those fuchsia cuttings. Fanny's coming to dinner."

"I know."

"Somebody will have to go, or they'll die, she'll say."

"I know. I see."

"There'll be chloral in your favorite drink tomorrow night."

"I know. I know."

"But then what? How can she work it?"

"I can't see any further," she confessed.

"How will she start the car? Be sure that it *is* started? And rig the doors? How *can* she?"

"There must be a way. It's what we don't know. It's what we—"

"Mandy, tomorrow you'll have to get out of here long enough to call Kelly."

"Why?"

"My God, to take care! Tell him he'll have to be down in the canyon. It'll be this way. In the first place, we'll see that you don't get any chloral. But she'll think you do. We'll have to take care of that. I'll ask for some liqueur too, as tonight. Somehow, we'll swap our glasses. If no chance comes up naturally, we'll have to make a chance. You make a chance, if you can. For me to do it. Turn her away for a second. I have an idea. I'll clear all the junk off that round table, the one with the revolving top. That'll be the way to do it. You manage to sit near and put your glass on that table. Remember. Mandy, will you trust me to swap those drinks?"

"Yes."

"Behind your back?"

"Yes, Thone. Yes, but you—"

"You must go ahead then, and drink yours, just as you always do. Mine won't matter because I can dawdle with it. She won't be thinking of mine or watching me. But listen, if it goes wrong and we're not able to swap them, then you must not leave the house. I won't allow it. I'll open up the whole thing before—"

"All right," she said.

"Mandy, is your heart O.K. ?"

"My h-heart?"

"Chloral's bad on a shaky heart. We won't go another step if there is the slightest chance."

"My heart's fine."

"Sure?"

"Yes, I'm sure."

"Doctor's word for it?"

"Yes, I have."

"What the hell am I talking about? Listen, Mandy, you'll get no chloral. Promise. Unless I say so, you mustn't drink anything at all."

"All right," she said numbly.

"Now, in case . . . Tell Kelly that somebody will have to be down there to watch how she does it, for one thing. You'll know, but we should have another witness. For another thing, to be sure you're not caught in there, after all, the way . . ." His head fell on his hands. . . . "the way Belle was."

Mandy shivered. Her throat was dry with pity, with terror.

He moved again. "Shall we call it off? I can't ask you to do this! My God, it's an impossible thing."

"We can't call it off," she said. "We don't know yet."

"We know, well enough."

"Not *how*."

"No *proof*." He groaned. She could feel his agony.

"What will I tell Mr. Kelly?" she prodded.

"To watch the garage. Keep listening. If he hears the car running with the doors closed, he's to break in. But not to call the house. We better not risk that. He mustn't be seen down there, either. Tell him early, tell him from eight on, to be sure."

"I touched the chloral box," she said.

"Did you?"

"I thought she was—wanting me to."

"Was she?"

"Oh, Thone, I don't know. I don't know. Are we scaring ourselves to death for nothing?"

"I don't think so. Mandy, can you walk into that trap? I wish it were the other way around."

"No, no. I'll be all right."

"Your hands are cold." He touched them.

"I'm freezing."

"If it weren't for—my mother . . ."

She lifted her face away from the cold metal bar. "There isn't really any danger," she said. "It isn't as if I were going to walk alone."

His fingers peeled hers off the bar and were warm around them. Then his whisper, so nearly soundless, "Nothing must happen to you, Amanda, Mandy." She thought, then, that although the words stopped, he said, "Darling."

"What—did you call me?" she murmured, bewildered.

He repeated, "Mandy."

She closed her eyes. No word, then. Yet he knew what word it was she hadn't heard with ears. The night was star-spangled. The night was perfumed. Her mouth, in the dark, was smiling.

Let him not speak, then. Neither would she.

She thought, not moving her lips, Good night, dear Thone.

"Good night," he whispered, answering.

18.

Mandy slept well and when she awoke it was Thursday. It was a misty morning. The long vistas were closed in. The canyon swooned in green and gray. Trees blurred and wept. The world was smaller. It was a small round clearing within a dreamy margin, a circle that moved and followed the eye, in which one walked and carried like a horizontal hoop the close horizon.

Tobias may have slept but he had not rested. His eyelids seemed barely able to lift and uncover his glance. He said he would do no work that day. No work at all.

So Mandy was free to sit and shiver in her white and yellow cotton. She told herself, after a while, that it was stupid to be chilly, and ran down to get her woolly jacket. When she came back, Tobias had gone to write in his room. Thone told her. Thone had hobbled to the sofa in the studio, and there he lay.

They looked at each other. There was much they could have whispered, had they dared. But nothing to say aloud, across the room. No words to match the normal crust of things, as around them the work of the house went on, all the housekeeping sounds. Elsie was busy. Ione, in the hall, spoke on the telephone to tradesmen, in gracious command.

Mandy went to sit on the window seat and stare out over the gardens that plunged so swiftly down into the misty gulch. She saw Burt, far below, digging in slow rhythm near the garage.

Thone put his eyes on a book. Ione glanced in.

In a little while Amanda saw her picking her way along the terraces below. No hat, but decent in a gray suit, with her purse under her arm. Was she going out?

Mandy turned. Was it safe? The vacuum hummed on the floor below. She pointed and grimaced.

"Give me the telephone," said Thone instantly.

She snatched it from its shelf in the hall. The long cord reached around the arch. "You keep on watching," he told her.

So she went back to the window seat. Ione was far below now, surely too far to hear the whir of the dial or the low rumble of Thone's voice. She was talking to Burt, who had stopped digging and listened respectfully.

She heard Thone ask for Lieutenant Kelly. Automatically, she filled in words from the other end of the wire. Lieutenant Kelly was not there. Thone was trying to leave a message. His low voice was staccato.

Below, Ione drew away from the gardener. He began to climb upward, dragging a tool. She opened the workshop door and went inside. The bottom of the canyon was not visible from the house, except at some distance, off toward the mouth of it, where a brief bare stretch of pavement could be seen. This morning the mist blurred it over. Mist, which was slowly dissolving in pale sunlight, but which lingered in the hollows below. If the car should pass that point on its way out, would it make a darker moving object? Amanda's eyes blinked with strain.

Thone hung up. He said, not very loud, but projecting the sound, "Kelly's not there. Where is she now?"

Amanda thought she saw something pass. "Gone out. Took the car, I think. I'm not sure."

He was getting up, reaching for the crutch. "Mandy, is there anybody you can ask? I'll be damned," he said, standing so close behind her that she could feel his voice vibrating in his chest, "if I'll trust your safety to a piece of paper on a cop's desk. Can't have him call back here. God knows if we'll get another chance. Messages don't always get delivered. He might not take it seriously. Can't let it go at that. Mandy, think of someone."

"There's Gene," she said. "He's—the chemist."

"Would he?"

"Yes."

"Then for God's sake, call him, now!" Thone hobbled a pace or two. "I'm going down there."

"Oh, no."

"Yes, I've got to see."

"I'll come too."

"No, no, you mustn't. You call. Get him. Get him! You know what to say. Make him swear to be there. He'll do that for you, won't he?"

"Yes," said Mandy.

"Then I'll go down. If she hasn't gone out, I can give you time. Hold her up. Make up a reason why I'm down there. But Mandy, if I can I want to see that place. Those door hooks."

"Can you walk enough?"

"Easily." He swung away. Turned his head. "Be careful. Remember Dad."

"I'll speak low," she said.

How did one telephone to Gene and explain that one expected to be murdered this evening and wouldn't he please come and watch! To a point . . . to any point at all!

Mandy called the Callahan number. She wouldn't ask for Kate. She couldn't risk her voice to Kate. Kate would catch it in one "hello," her fear, her excitement. Gene was different. He knew a little more. He knew about the poison. She saw her strategy.

"Gene? It's Mandy. I have to talk very fast and you must listen. Remember the test you made for me?"

"Yeah?"

"Something like that . . . up here. Will you be what you said, if ever I needed . . ."

"Bodyguard!" His voice was suddenly louder and alarmed.

"Tonight, by eight o'clock, be in the lower road below this house. Abermarle Road, it is. Off Linda Vista. Almost all the way to the end there is a garage in the hillside, on the left. Gene, please be there to watch what happens. It may—catch somebody. Do you understand?"

"The one who fixed it before?" He was cautious.

"Yes. Don't be seen. It has to go far enough. Will you believe me, Gene, and do what I say?"

"Sure, Mandy."

"Notice everything. Don't—do anything, unless the doors stay closed or are closed again and the car is running inside. If it gets that far, then raise a row and get in."

"Uh-huh," he said. "Who am I likely to find in there? This son? This attractive chocolate drinker?"

"That's it," said Mandy.

"And where will you be?"

"I'll be watching from here," she murmured.

"Does the guy know what he's in for?"

"Yes, yes, and he'll be careful. But something might go wrong. Gene, will you promise?"

"You don't make much sense. You know that?"

"I can't make sense," she wailed. "I haven't got time. Quick, say you will!"

"Anything you say."

"Oh, Gene, you're—"

"Yeah," he said, "sure I am. How are you, honey?"

"Fine. I'm fine." She steadied her voice, raised it to cheerfulness.

"Coming home—lessee—tomorrow?"

"Yes, tomorrow."

"See you," said Gene, "anyhow, then."

"But tonight—you surely will?" she whispered.

"Surely. Surely. Don't worry. So if nothing happens?"

"Then tomorrow I'll try to thank you."

"Yeah," he said. "O.K."

She put up the phone, rested her mouth on her wrist. If he knew it was her danger, he'd interfere. He'd bust the pattern, if it was a pattern, wide-open. He'd have none of it. Therefore, she had lied.

What a delicate web it was! Cobweb and countercobweb. Now, in this misty morning, with the vacuum humming in the quiet house, it was a cobweb of fantasy, spun out of nothing, unreal, impossible, a phantom structure. So tenuous and subtle, so unlinked to the earth, to that which was solid, to the flesh or the fact . . .

She moved her mouth on the skin of her hand. Her mind went down around the path again. Belle was dead. In a web of strange construction, she'd been caught and she had died. If mere blind chance had woven it, could blind chance duplicate? Or had there been a spider, after all?

Now, here, one thought one saw all these duplicating threads, repeating the pattern. But perhaps it was a cobweb that drifted in air, silken, invisible, spun in the mind. . . .

Yet it *was* anchored! It *did* swing from one point. In *one* place, it was glued to reality. There had been poison in the chocolate. A chocolate cobweb, she thought, half hysterically. It's a chocolate cobweb. . . .

19.

Thone swung down the stairs. He traveled fast, one hand on the banister, one on the crutch. His right foot throbbed a little as it swung free, but it didn't impede him. He went out the lower door into the air.

On the slope he moved more slowly. Half his mind revolved, thinking what to say, how to explain, if he should meet her. The rest of it was a blur of anxiety, a blind urge to do something, to push at the subtle threads, either to touch and realize them or to brush them away as nothing. He could not—could not—any longer sit on that sofa and watch the girl's face. Watch her drift with dumb courage, with that look of singularly sweet, dumb, passive, unprotesting courage.

Burt, at the far end of the first terrace, looked up and exclaimed.

"Tired of the damn house." Thone threw him this and it was enough. Burt's face wrinkled in a grin. He saluted. Thone went on down. Burt, trimming edges, worked on and up around the corner of the house.

Alone, unseen, Thone descended. Toward this place, this small dug-in building of unimportant stone and stucco. This shrine! Ah, if Belle had been murdered, then it was no shrine. It was evil's altar, and she the sacrifice.

He drew nearer the door. The workshop hadn't been there in his mother's day. It was part of his father's new wall. This new door was the true gate of the fortress that kept his father's privacy.

He stood on his good left foot. Close to the door and staring at it, he could see that it was not quite shut all the way. It rested on the tongue of the lock. It looked closed but it was not.

Then, as he stood there, it began to move.

Down in the workshop, Ione nudged the key with the toe of her shoe, a little closer to the heap of burlap sacks Burt saved there in the corner. She looked at it, tilting her white head thoughtfully. No, it would gleam. It would catch light. Especially a flashlight's beams. She moved it with her toe until it slid under a fold of the burlap. Only a little way under, of course. The metal fastener on which the key still hung made a tiny sound on the metal of the key itself. The fastener would seem to have slipped out of the groove in her key case. (It could happen, she thought. It has happened.) There. Quite hidden, but not too well.

Detail.

She glanced around the small dusty place. Footprints? Ah, no bother. Everyone came through here, often. Especially herself. Fingerprints? No, none, except on the doorknobs, where they were quite natural.

None at all, no trace of fingers on the little button in the edge of the middle door. The little button one had only to push to set the old lock working. The little button that was never set so, for reasons of convenience. But that was set so now.

Before the days of the workshop and the wall, this middle door had functioned as a barrier. It could, still. Although the key to it was hanging there on a nail, where it had hung for years, inside the workshop, lest one be trapped.

Lest one be trapped.

She would not touch it. Not that key. Let it hang there, representing safety. If one knew of it. If one did not know of it, why, it was hidden well enough.

No fingerprints. Quite so.

She had rubbed the ax handle with one of the sacks. The ax was lying on the floor now, as if it had fallen over. It was covered with dirt. Burt hadn't used it for a long time. It would seem that no one had.

The gas pipe was worked loose at its fittings, there near the floor in the far corner. It hadn't taken many blows. She'd muffled the ax head in burlap to pound at it. First, to deaden sound. Although Burt would not hear. He was a trifle deaf. And sound was deceptive in the canyon. It bounced and echoed from the steep banks and its place of origin was never clear. Second, she'd muffled it so there would be no marks. And there were none that she could see.

The pipe, coming in here, from outside, had moved in the wall, and in the earth beyond, she supposed. Where she had directed Burt to dig this morning. His spade would have glanced on the metal of the pipe, perhaps. Indeed, she hoped it had. For, of course, it would seem that he had dislodged this old unused gas outlet, which was too dangerous to use here in the small room, not easily ventilated any more, since the glass brick band had been put across the wall.

How fortunate that she'd found the sight of all this junk distressing from the garden, and only three months ago had taken steps. . . .

The gas, of course, was turned off up above. From the house. She'd attended to that. It could be made to flow again, so simply.

However, she thought complacently, if matters did not fall out as she expected and hoped, if all did not go quite smoothly, why, the gas would never flow at all. No one would ever know of these preparations.

Ah, but if it went well, it would be a mystery! Of the human heart, the human mind. . . . The romantic story of a young girl, all lost in her dream of this beautiful and unknown mother, so tragically dead. And a young girl, furthermore, hopelessly in love with inscrutable, cool, polite, and distant Thone. Who was so charming. So famously charming. (For it could happen. It had happened. That other girl had died, had done it, and on Thone's innocent account. This was a fact, and known. So convincing, history.)

So it would be part explained, part mystery. Amanda would take the drug herself, of course, under the spell of the old story. A single dose, as Belle had done. Not a lethal dose, no, it might be too violent, too soon. She was afraid of violence and of company. This must happen apart, afar, in loneliness and mystery, shrouded and guessed at. . . . No, it would seem she had planned to be found exactly as the mother had been found. The mother whose painted likeness made her weep.

And if Fate stepped in and trapped her a little differently, if there was an accidental variation . . . Ah, who would guess or even begin to guess that it was only because the trick had to be worked from the house this time. And there was no way, no way Ione could think of, although she'd tried so hard, to work it quite the same.

Still, she felt satisfied. She felt, in fact, a pleasant excitement. There was no need to hate Amanda now. Indeed, she'd forgotten to hate, forgotten to suffer with it, in the quite absorbing business of making these little arrangements.

Ah, no need to suffer. She shrugged, smiling. Yes, it would go along, much as before, with a way open to change one's mind and back out at every point. Since her plan seized and used so much pure chance, no one would ever see a plan at all. In this lay her safety. In this, her great cleverness! She was not much concerned about the police. They would, of course, appear.

She thought, since Tobias would be grieving, she would devote herself to his comforting. So she would be occupied. Let the police come and go. She would be nursing him and have little to say. Unless it were necessary to touch and guide them to an appreciation of the tragic dream in the silly young head. Still, Fanny would tell them about that. And Thone . . . And even those girls at the party.

She sighed. No, she was not much concerned about the police. They had come and gone before. She had not even been at the inquest. As far as she knew, it had never entered their heads to consider . . .

She had no name for what she did.

One more detail, she thought. To go through the garden door, which lay gently poised on the tongue of the lock so that she could get through from this side, and yet leave her key where it nestled under the sacks; go through and close the garden door behind her and take Burt off, out of the gardens now, lest he discover, in some rambling aimless manner, that the lock was on the middle door. No, he must go away with Elsie, now, to wherever servants went on their day.

She turned to the garden door and pulled it open. And saw Thone's back, as there he stood, leaning on his crutch, not four feet away.

"Thone, dear! How you startled me! Good heavens!" She gasped to breathe.

He turned his face. He looked startled, too. "Sorry, Ione."

"How long—a way you've come, dear! How could you have walked all this way down? Is there something you wanted? You might have sent Burt. Were you coming in here, dear?" She revised all her plans, undid them in a second. "What is it? Can I help you?"

"Oh, no," he said, "there wasn't anything."

"But Thone." Her breath was a little easier. Her mind buzzed craftily. "If you came all this way down, surely it was for something?"

He said wearily, "Were you out, Ione? I didn't know where you were."

Had he heard anything?

"I ran to the drugstore," she lied. "How I must have startled you!"

"You sure did," he murmured.

No, no, he hadn't heard anything. She let the door move, cau-

tiously, tentatively. If he went in—and if he tried the middle door
. . . She must not seem to mind whether he went in. If he did . . .
But if he did not . . . The plan alternately swelled and faded. It
wavered, all unsure.

Thone said, letting his voice show violence, absorbed in his
own scheme to deceive, "I had to get away from that girl!"

"Oh, Thone." She let the door slip shut, very gently. She peered
at his face. "Why, dear? What has she done?"

"Nothing," he said painfully. "Dad's writing letters. We were
left—alone."

"Poor boy," she murmured. "It must be so distressing, her feeling for you."

"Don't talk about it." He slashed at a shrub with his crutch.

"No, dear." Now the door was shut. "We must have Burt to
help you up. You will go, since I'm back?"

"I suppose so." He hobbled a little way on the path.

"Try to be patient," said Ione softly behind him. "I don't think
Amanda will be here much longer."

"I—know." He straightened his shoulders.

Ione was quite pleased. He felt as she wished him to feel. It
fitted in well. She made as if to firm the door. A little gesture
of finality. All here was left as she wished it to be left. The plan
would hold. So far. And all was tidy.

She called out rather merrily to Burt and he came around
the corner of the house and hurried down. Thone went up between them less easily than he had descended. As they entered
the house, he was speaking, rather loudly. (Mandy must not be
on the telephone. Mandy must hang up.) "I can't bear the way she
looks at me!" he cried. "God knows I try to be polite . . ."

"Ah, hush," said Ione.

Mandy was curled in a chair with a book. She lifted her head. Tobias was coming out of his room into the hall. She couldn't hear the words but she heard voices and saw Tobias freeze for a moment. She knew they were coming.

She took air into her lungs. And let it go slowly and shakily. Ah, but now, she thought, this part of the time, these hours are the worst. I'm in the thick of the worst of it. Now is the time to be steady.

And she put the book down and smiled greeting, as a pretty guest should, just before lunch, on a lazy, peaceful, quite unremarkable Thursday morning.

20.

The dining room of the canyonside house was on the northwest, with a semicircle of glass for the outer wall. There they supped, by candlelight. But the curtains were not drawn and they saw the day die, far off on the mountaintops, where it had lingered later than here. Thursday was slipping to the west. It would be over the ocean. Soon gone to sea.

The meal was very informal, since there was no Elsie to cook or serve it. Ione, at the foot of the table, filled their plates from a huge casserole and an even larger salad bowl. She handled the serving spoons with dainty pride. Bolt upright she sat, in a dull lavender silk frock, crisply set off by a little white ruching. Her white hair was heaped high, showing her small ears, which wore tonight tiny amethyst buttons in the lobes. Amethyst beads, in an old-fashioned design, lay close around her soft neck, on the soft, pale, delicately wrinkled flesh that would be clean and scented. Her cheeks were pink, doll pink, on the round of the bones. Her dark eyes were pleased and sparkling in the candlelight.

So cute, she looked! Cute, adorable little old Mrs. Santa Claus, with such pink, clean, brisk, and busy little hands!

Fanny, like a raddled old parrot who had fought age to a draw and now ignored the whole matter with a kind of brilliant indifference, was in shining black. She wore her diamonds.

Amanda's dress was a simple, soft thing, with nothing remarkable about it except its color. It was crimson, rich red, a jewel color, so brilliant, lush, and startling in itself that she was less a girl than a flame to the eye. It hid her. It picked her up and put her so brazenly in view, so flamboyantly and conspicuously burning there, that, in a sense, she was not seen. Tobias couldn't keep his eyes off it. He could not look away. The color seemed to brace him. He was not quite so weary and spent in its reflected glow.

Thone, at her left, as the two of them faced Fanny, was shut off and closed away. He'd hardly turned his eyes toward Mandy. Communication was dead between them, as if all wires were cut. As they must be, she knew.

There had been one code message, however. A question asked and answered, before supper, when Thone, glancing casually at the evening paper, had muttered what seemed an aimless comment. "These chemists! What'll they do next?"

And Mandy had murmured, as carelessly as she could, "Oh, they'll discover something startling. They're always working. Night and day."

He hadn't replied, as if he snubbed this friendly response. Fanny had picked it up. "I hope they get around to rejuvenation before it's too late. I would be spitting mad, let me tell you, if I missed it by one generation. I'd like to be Amanda's age again. By gum, I would!"

"Oh, I don't know, Fanny," Ione had said piously. "I think we forgot how youth can suffer."

"Good for 'em," snapped Fanny. "Did you ever read—"

Fanny did most of the talking.

That made it easier to sit here now, with supper nearly over and the evening upon them. To sit here in a crimson frock, listening, nodding, smiling, eating, playing the pretty young guest at the table. But really waiting. And certain, now, quite finally certain now, what it was she waited for.

Ione had spoken, in the kitchen, as Mandy, in one of Elsie's big aprons, had helped as a young guest should. Mandy, breaking lettuce with her fingers, had received the expected and been braced for it. Thone didn't know yet, but she knew. She was proud to think that her hands had gone right on. Nothing had happened to her breathing. Something had happened deep inside, a little click of the mind, and then a flowing relief, as if to know, for sure, was going to be easier and even heartening. As if the courage that had been strained, waiting to be used, was released to function, to exist, to take hold now, and let her smile . . . go headlong the way she was being pushed to go, and make it easy.

Ione had begun, "Oh, my dear! I'm afraid I'm supposed to be at the airport! I shouldn't . . . But it would be such a shame . . . Oh, what a pity," Ione had mourned, "to let those lovely cuttings die!"

"Couldn't I go?" Amanda had asked. So sweet, so willing.

21.

They stacked the dishes, Fanny applauding. It was getting late when they came, at last, into the studio. Tobias was in his favorite chair. Fanny poked up the fire to a brisker blaze, saying she did like a fire, although she retreated at once to a far chair with its back to the length of the room beyond, and sat on her foot and fingered her diamonds.

Mandy drifted near one of the two chairs that flanked the small round table and stood there, hesitating politely, watching her hostess. Ione had brought with her from the kitchen a tumbler of milk. She said cozily, "I'll just fetch us all something. Toby, dear, I think you really must . . . Come help me, Amanda."

Thone had hobbled to the wide window. He had pulled the cord that drew the curtains together. Now he stood, still, leaning on the crutch, holding a hem of the neutral-colored stuff with one hand to make a gap, as if he looked to see how the night had fallen before he let the curtain drop and shut it out.

Ione turned on a lamp over the little bar in the corner. "Fanny, dear, will you have what we're having?"

"Anything," said Fanny moodily. She was watching her dear

friend Tobias, whose head lay on the chair, whose face was white and tired. "Something troubles you, Toby?" she asked softly.

"No, Fan. No." He opened his eyes at her and it was as if her words had put alarm there. He looked haunted for a second.

Back of the bar, Ione took down the chloral. Carefully, she dosed the milk, shaking the powder from its fold of paper while Amanda stood and watched her.

The fire sputtered.

"Thone?" Ione's right hand went to the familiar bottle. "The same, dear?"

"The same," he answered dreamily, not turning. Ione lifted the bottle, judged its remaining contents, nodded and smiled at Amanda. And Mandy's lips drew easily into the answering smile. Ione took down glasses, four dainty stemmed glasses. She filled one.

"I'll just take Toby his," she said. "Will you pour some for the rest of us, my dear?" She took the milk and one liqueur.

Amanda moved around behind the bar. She looked stupidly after Ione's back. It bent graciously to her guest. "Fanny?" Then to her husband. "Now, drink this, Toby." The little paw touched his tired head in a brief caress.

Fanny sniffed at her glass and snorted. But she said no word. Amanda stifled a gasp and picked up the bottle. Obediently, in that drifting yet stubborn do-as-you're-told state, she poured three glasses full of the liqueur. It sparkled and winked at her.

Thone seemed to moon at the night with an unfocused gaze. But he did not. His eyes were focused and alert. He could see the bar, the shelf behind it, the glasses, the whole lit corner reflected in the window glass. He saw Amanda take a drink up in either hand.

Ione had timed it neatly. She was trotting back. The plump little lady, the slender girl met, crossed paths. "That's right, my dear," said Ione. "Thone? Aren't you going to sit down?"

"Um . . . put it on the table," he murmured. He seemed to fumble with the crutch. It stuttered on the carpet. The curtain trembled in his hand, but did not fall yet.

Back of the bar, Ione, as she quickly and precisely shook one dose into the fourth and only remaining glass of liqueur, seemed to be fussily busy at making all neat, at putting the drug away. Thone let the curtain go, very gently. It settled softly and hid the mirror in which he had seen what he had been waiting for. A single dose. He'd seen. Now he was sure.

It was the second time, he thought quite calmly, she'd been watched in a window glass. She had a blind spot there. She didn't seem to know it could make a mirror.

He swung around. Mandy had put one glass on the round table. She stood, holding the other in her hand. She half turned. Ione was coming around the bar with a bright fixed smile on her jolly little face, and nothing at all in her hands. Oh, it was neat. It was deft. It was so simple. For one did not call out to one's elder and hostess, "Hey, you left yours on the bar!" One murmured, as Mandy did, "Shall I put yours here?" One put it on the end table near the sofa corner, Ione's corner. One minded one's manners if one had been well brought up. Quite so.

They met. They crossed for the second time. "Thanks, dear." Ione touched the girl's arm. In gratitude. For the fourth glass waited, on the bar, and Amanda went to get it.

"This must be mine," said she cheerfully.

Thone checked the stiffening of his jaw muscles. He moved to stand behind the table. No one could tell whether Amanda knew what she held in her hand, what she carried so steadily down the room. She walked past Fanny and went, smiling, to the chair near Tobias. She put the little glass down on the round tabletop, at her left. She drew up her knees and clasped her hands around them and sat, as Belle used to sit, as she herself now sat so often.

Fanny looked on sourly. Fanny turned her own glass, by its stem, round and round.

Ione settled into her sofa corner, and her little feet dangled, not quite touching the floor. Thone moved around, sat down, and on opposite sides of the bare round tabletop, their two glasses, his and Mandy's, rested between them.

Ione lifted her drink. She twinkled at them, at the young people. "Come, Thone, drink your drink. Here's to us!" she chirped. She sipped. Her eyes, as she sipped, did not cease watching.

How had it happened? How was it that they sat here, pinned in her full view, so helplessly side by side under those unwavering dark and wary eyes? Thone's hand picked up his glass. Had to. He looked down at its innocence glumly.

"What's that you're all drinking?" asked Tobias suddenly.

"Just a liqueur, Toby," soothed Ione. Fanny's lips tightened but she said nothing.

There was such tension here, the silences, the intervals were screaming. As if all their nerves were tightening, like strings, and screaming with the strain. Tobias' chest felt heavy. He had begun to feel as if somewhere at the back of his skull there'd be a cracking. His brain was far behind his intuition. It was lost. His thought churned helplessly. A group of people by the fire, after dinner. Nothing. Then, why . . . ?

Ione said, glancing daintily at her wrist, "I wonder if it isn't nearly time, Amanda, dear. You mustn't be out too late, you know. I think, perhaps . . ." The head nodded, indicating, instructing.

"Of course," Amanda said. She unclasped her hands. Her feet came to the floor. Her fingers went to the stem of her glass. Had to pick it up. Had to obey.

Take it. Touch it to your lips. All's ready. All is prepared. Drink it, touch it, and go and die.

Thone sat like a statue. Too bad. Too bad. Here the whole ragged business must fall apart. Now plot and counterplot must go no further. Ah, so close. To know so much, and now to fail. But he couldn't let Amanda take the stuff! Not really. No. That mouth toward which the rim of the glass was moving, that lovely mouth, must never touch it!

Tobias said hoarsely. "Why, where's Amanda going?"

"On a little errand," said Ione lightly. Then to Amanda, "You'll want the car, dear, won't you? Can you find the keys?"

His eyes started—Tobias' eyes—from his head. His hand jerked. The milk slopped over. It dribbled on his trousers. The tumbler slipped out of his slackening hold and fell on the rug.

22.

Ione cried out. Amanda put her drink, gladly, quickly, on the tabletop, and slipped out of her chair, crouching to snatch at the rolling tumbler.

"Here, take my handkerchief," said Thone calmly. "Ah, too bad."

"Toby, dear!" Ione was alarmed.

Tobias was looking down at Mandy's soft hair, at her pretty back, the rich glow of her dress, at her hand scrubbing spilled milk with Thone's handkerchief. "I'm terribly sorry," he said, quite normally. His eyes turned in his head. He thought, None of them notice! None of them remember. I must not speak now of Belle. For none of them realize this echoing. It's a coincidence. Only to me is it all so horribly the same.

Fanny was plain furious. Her eyes licked angrily at Mandy's back. "You'd better have your stuff that helps you sleep, Toby, and get to bed. You're jittery. You need to rest. You must have rest." She switched her wrathful gaze to Thone.

"I'll fetch more milk," said Ione, with a wild worried look around. She hurried away. Her little feet pattered nervously. She almost ran.

Mandy, on her knees, mopped at the spot. Tobias, pinching his trouser leg, half rose out of the chair. Fanny was glaring. "I can't drink this stuff!" she said.

But Thone gave no heed to Fanny. He put his glass of Herbsaint on Mandy's side of the table. He took up the drink that had been prepared for her. He held it, as he had been holding his own. He sat quite still and his mouth slipped into a small, strangely triumphant little smile.

Fanny said, in a low strangling voice, "Thone, in God's name . . ."

He lifted his eyes. Fanny's face, so trained, so practiced, so able to show what she felt, showed now her perfect astonishment. Then fear. Bewilderment, then pain. Then panic.

Ah, no! He groaned inside. His smile vanished. All trace of it went out of his consciousness. Fanny would blurt out something. Fanny would say, would ask. Fanny had seen what he did and she was going to spoil it yet! Now! Now that he had succeeded. Now that Mandy was safe and all was well and it could proceed. Now that he had the danger here in his hand, and Gene waited in the canyon and they would so soon know. . . . He fastened his eyes on hers. He moved his lips. He made faces that said, Hush, hush.

It was no use. Fanny was going to spoil it all, unless he could . . . He juggled the crutch. He put the glass down to grasp it. No, he could not get up and go to her. It was too awkward. He beckoned, instead.

Fanny obeyed. She got up and came toward him, drawn, fascinated, willing, for just this moment, to be silent and listen.

Mandy, kneeling, still scrubbed. She was speaking some reassuring words about the stain.

Thone turned in the chair, caught at Fanny's arm. The henna head came down. He whispered, "Be still. Let it go. I'll tell you later. Fanny, if you love me . . ."

And in this moment, Tobias, half standing, pinching the trouser leg still with his left hand, took his trembling right forefinger and turned the table. Turned the round revolving tabletop. Quietly, unseen by anyone, unseen by Mandy, crouching there, unseen by the two who were whispering so frantically, unseen by Ione, now hurrying back, it slipped around. The glasses, in a stately figure, like an old dance, followed each other on the turning rim. They changed places.

Mandy said, "There, I think that does it." She sat on her heels.

A mask slipped over Fanny's face. She glided past Thone and leaned as if to inspect. "Yes, child, I should think so."

Ione, pattering in, caught them as they were posed in her dark glance. She said cheerily, "No harm done. None at all. I'll have this for you in a minute, Toby dear." Tobias fell into the chair as she carried his fresh milk to the bar. Mandy got up.

"For heaven's sake," said Thone, squirming irritably, "sit down, everybody. Drink your drink, Mandy. Elsie can clean that, can't she?"

"Why, of course she can," said Ione quite gaily. "Mustn't cry over spilled milk, anyhow." She trilled her laughter.

Tobias lay as he had fallen. He was ill—ill. . . . No one must leave this house, having drunk from a dubious glass. No one. That was the impulse. But ah—he was ill. He was not clear in his head. He was somehow entangled with the past. He was not seeing clearly.

Thone, whom he called in his heart The Boy, as if he were

the only best boy, the whole generation of wonderful male youth distilled in this boy, his dear own— Thone could have meant no harm. It was nothing that he'd changed so swiftly, in so slick a fashion, one glass for another under Tobias' startled eyes. No, it meant nothing. It could mean nothing.

He could not have put any alien substance in one of those glasses. Not Thone! Ah, no! Never!

One had only to wait and see this proved before his eyes. How meaningless it was. For Thone would drink of the wrong glass and remain here, and take it in this room. And he, Tobias, would observe how nothing happened, and he would know himself to have been an old fool. A terrified old fool, worked on by memories, putting past horror into present . . . nothings.

For Thone would not wish to injure Mandy, sweet pretty Mandy. What Tobias had heard him saying could not apply to Mandy. Not bear to have her look at him? Resent her here? Not Thone, who had his mother's generous heart. Not Thone, who was surely, surely . . . Oh, what a fool I am! Not so small as to hate, not so narrow as to resent, not so stupid as to strike out, blind and angry . . .

Ah, if he was cool to this pretty child, it was only because of that old affair, the other girl who'd wounded and frightened him so that he never quite dared be himself. Tobias could understand. He knew all this. He knew it well. He knew The Boy.

He was sorry, now, that he'd so impulsively changed the glasses around again. He regretted his panic, that brief loss of faith. He should have had faith!

In The Boy. This man . . . grown and so long away . . .

He began to shudder. Ah, God, but he lacked . . . He had no

faith . . . since she'd left him. He was lost, lost, since she'd taken her life away. He had understood nothing since. Nothing. And he was nothing, since she'd gone so enigmatically, so cruelly, cruelly, out of the world. He was only a nervous, shattered old fool, who should have died, not hereafter, but herebefore. . . .

"Toby, my dear! You're having a chill!"

Ah, empty and lost was he, with only Ione to cling to now. "I don't know," he said. "Ione, I don't know."

"Take it easy, Dad," said Thone quietly.

The shuddering stopped.

"There, dearest. Your milk." Ione hovered over him. "He'll be all right," she told the rest.

Amanda took her glass, sighing.

"Of course he will," said Fanny. Her face was smooth but her body seemed to huddle in the chair.

23.

Amanda felt easier. She knew it was going to be all right now. Soon she could get up and go out of this room, and for her the worst would be over. At least she would be alone. She would not have to smile and smile and keep her muscles slack when they fought to tighten. She sipped at her drink.

She thought, What fear can do! She thought it tasted very especially strong and nasty. If she hadn't known, as Thone had told her, by their code, when he'd said to drink it . . . If she hadn't known he meant her to do just that . . . She fought not to wrinkle her face and close her throat against the stuff. Well, it was the last time, the very last time she'd ever try to down this Herbsaint and pretend she liked it.

Of course, he'd done it when the milk was spilled. She'd turned her back and fussed over Tobias and the spot, to help all she could. She knew, vaguely, it was the total tension that had upset Tobias and made him drop his glass. But there was no time to think too much about that.

A little minute, now, to choke this down, ignoring the dark eyes she could feel, sly, upon her. And then to leave. Escape and breathe and go down and permit in the lonely dark a heartbeat or two, or a nervous tightening of the hand.

She drank it as quickly as she could and rose with a burning throat. "I'd better go."

"Yes, dear. They'll be in the checkroom in my name. The keys are in the hall, Amanda."

"I must say good night." Amanda made her manners. "Good night, Miss Austin. Good night, Mr. Garrison—all."

"Good night," said Fanny shortly. Tobias gave her only a wan smile. She was a crimson blur to his eyes.

Thone said easily, "I'd ride along but this damned foot . . . You'll have to excuse me."

"Oh, please don't come," said Mandy, almost too quickly.

"I'll put the floodlights on in the garden," said Ione pleasantly. "But take my flash, too, dear. You mustn't stumble."

"Oh, I won't stumble," sang Amanda joyously. "Good night. Good night."

To get away would be so good!

She walked around the sofa, up the one step, took the keys off the hall table and the black flashlight, snatched her woolly jacket from where it lay on a chair, and her purse. Ione had followed.

"I shall wait up," said that little lady gently. The dark eyes were pitying and almost kind.

"Thank you."

"Thank you, my dear. You're very sweet to do this for me."

Amanda managed one last smile. She put her feet on the stairs.

Ione listened to the nervous haste of her descending footsteps. Then she went briskly through the kitchen to turn on . . . the floodlights.

Deep in the canyon, Gene Noyes leaned on the trunk of a sycamore. He had left his car back a ways, near enough to somebody's house to count as if he'd gone in there. Walking farther into this gulch, he'd spotted the garage easily enough. He gazed at the white blot it made in the darkness. He wanted to smoke but thought he'd better not. He could just see the lighted house from here, where he leaned at the far side of the lower road. But not much of the slope leading down. The wall and the treetops hid the lower part of it.

It was chilly, waiting there. But he had not waited long when he saw the lights go on. Suddenly, floodlights, shooting down from the corners of the house, made day-bright the terraces, the steps, the paths. Foliage and flower sprang into exquisite and uncanny beauty. Gene saw only the upper bit of this fairyland. The rest was just a glow from beyond the wall.

He drew deeper under the tree. Then he saw that a car was mooching slowly along the lower road toward him, coming very softly and with dimmed lights. It was a police car.

Ducking and dodging along the far margin of the road, he ran to meet it. "Wait," he said, panting. "Listen."

The car seemed to listen. At least, it stopped. Lieutenant Kelly put his head out. "Who are you?"

"I'm supposed to be watching. You?"

"Garrison's?"

"Yeah."

"Yeah," said Kelly. "What the hell?"

"I dunno," said Gene. "Lights just went on. Maybe you'd better . . ."

The car seemed to pussyfoot backward, withdrawing daintily as a cat. "Thought I saw somebody come outa the house," murmured the driver as he turned his head.

"Yeah?" Kelly peered upward. Whatever it was, he'd missed it. "Gimme the story," he demanded.

"Mandy—Amanda Garth—"

"I know her."

"—called me," said Gene, swallowing surprise. "There's something screwy going on up there. Woman wants to—uh—do in this son. Or so she told me."

"Son, eh?"

"Yeah. In the garage. If the motor's running I'm supposed to—"

"I know all about that."

"Well, I don't," said Gene. "Mandy thinks they're going to catch her in the act or something."

"Goddamn crazy kids!" said Kelly in disgust. "What are you going to do?" It wasn't a question. It was a remark.

Gene shrugged. They looked up toward the glow.

"Wait a while," said Kelly to his driver. "Then we'll run up closer and take a look. Wait and see if those lights go out. Meantime, better douse ours."

The driver turned the switch. The car settled in darkness. Gene leaned on the fender. "Maybe I oughta work back a little nearer," he said nervously.

"Hold it."

"What?"

"She's supposed to come down here and fix the doors."

"Oh."

"So let her," said Kelly grimly, "if she's going to. Personally, I'd be surprised."

From this distance, their three pair of eyes watched the faint white shimmer of those double doors. The night was quiet. Once they thought they heard something unnatural. But sound behaved oddly, down here. They looked up the slope behind them. And there was nothing there, of course.

Mandy came out of the lower door. She shivered in the night air. Her face felt hot—no, not hot. Cold. Her brain felt fuzzy. The sudden relief, she thought, was making her feel so queer. She tried to catch her breath and hurry along. She couldn't seem to draw air in, not deep enough.

But the rest was simple. All she had to do was just go down, do as she was told, make all the motions, go all the way to meet whatever was coming. Maybe even, at some well-chosen moment, pretend to faint? She thought, Oh, God, I'm terrified. I've never been so scared in all my life. Yet her heart was not fast. It seemed, instead, slower and slower.

She bit her lips. She must get there. It would never do to faint, really, faint too soon from this sickening fear. It would never do to collapse now. Weakly, out of plain terror. No. It will pass, she told herself. It will pass.

The way to conquer it was to do what she must do and ignore the feelings. She concentrated. The path was clear in the light. She did not stumble.

24.

Thone put the glass of liqueur on the table. Let it stand there, ready to accuse her when the time came.

Right now, in the next few minutes, was the time to watch. This was the crucial time. She must act. She must complete the pattern.

What would Ione do? Would she remember some letters to mail? Would she go for a handkerchief? Would she excuse herself and state no reason and let them assume it was unmentionable?

She was still out beyond the kitchen. Or was she?

He wished he could go to the arch and peer across. He could not move from the chair, of course. His foot . . . No reason. He sent Fanny a grin but he scarcely saw her.

Mandy was on her way down through the gardens now. Right now. He thought, That chemist of hers better be there. Minutes beat past.

Where was Ione? What was she doing? Had she slipped out of the house already? Was it going to be as simple as that?

He had to know. He got out of the chair.

In the service porch, Ione strained with her cheek on the pane to see past the bulge of the dining room, looking down. That brief flash of the red skirt, crossing the slope there. That was she! How lucky that color! There, it crossed again, zigzagging the other way. She was moving down steadily. She was drawing near. . . .

All that was necessary, now, was that she go through that door, that first door.

All that was necessary, now. And it flew on the rim of the wheel of chance. The wheel would soon settle to a stop. Would the drug pull her down too soon? Or would she first reach and go through that door? Ah, let there be one last bit of smooth going, one last acquiescence of fate, and then . . .

She saw the red of the skirt, far down. She saw it vanish. She did not draw breath until she thought she could discern, across the back of the workshop, a pale gleam outlining and squaring the corners of the band of glass brick, from inside.

She put a towel over her hand, and then the hand on the valve for gas. It turned hard. But it turned.

Then she tossed the towel down the laundry chute, where it would sail to the washroom in the basement.

She worked her fingers. She touched her amethyst earrings. Ah, poor Toby, she thought sadly. Ah, poor dear Toby. I must be strong for him. He will need me so desperately.

She heard the crutch thud on the linoleum floor of the kitchen behind her. Her hand went to the switch for the floodlights. She turned her head, easily, to look at him in mild surprise, over her shoulder. He came on, in his limping rhythm. "A glass of water," he said glumly.

"Dear, you should have called," she chided. She pushed the

switch and the glow beyond the windows faded instantly. Light still shone from the workshop wall. All had gone well. She wrenched her attention, all of it, inside the house. She bustled from the service porch to the kitchen water cooler.

"I can wait on myself," said Thone irritably. "I'm not a cripple." He came to the cooler.

Ione withdrew, delicately. "I'm sorry," she said. "I'm afraid I just like to fuss, you know." He was so tall. She had to arch her neck. "It's the way I am," she sighed. Her fingers played with the amethysts around her throat.

Thone, looking down, thought, What way are you?

He couldn't understand. He began to feel a strange declining, falling feeling, a definite letdown.

Mandy tucked her purse under her arm and fumbled with the key case. She found a key of the proper size by its feel. Before she could try it, the door moved inward under the light pressure of her other hand on the knob. She had forgotten. She juggled the flashlight and found the button on it. If there was a light switch here in the workshop she didn't know where. The beam came on and trembled over the floor.

She stepped in and the door, pressed by its own spring as she stepped around it and let it go, fell softly and yet heavily shut behind her.

She realized that the strange weakening terror in her veins had not departed. It was on her now. It was in her throat. It blurred her vision. She could not deepen her breath. It seemed to hiss in her ears.

Her nostrils quivered. Surely there was a faint odor of gas in this place.

The light wavered to the middle door. She went, weakly, shuffling like someone very old, across the small space. Her fear was, as yet, fixed on a point beyond that middle door. But it would not open. She put both hands on the knob and turned and tugged. It would not open. It must be locked. She worked at the key case. Her hands were shaking so that she almost could not hold it at all. She tried the key.

She felt very queer. Something was hissing behind her. It was not in her head. The key wouldn't fit. Nor would the only other key of the right size. There was no key!

Go back! Get out!

Fear, like a goblin, fear, like a ghost, seeped through the wall, oozed through the tight brick to this side of it. The fear was right here in the workshop. It was all around her.

The hissing sound was gas escaping.

Go back! Get out!

She stumbled to the garden door. It had shut. It had locked.

The keys chattered in her hand. She pulled herself together, sternly, with a surge of desperate courage.

But there was no key. Among these keys, there was no right key. The keys in her hand were of no use at all.

Locked in? Turn off that gas, then! Quickly! She followed sound to the corner. At the last she was crawling. But there was nothing to turn. The leak was not from a tap. Her hands were of no use. No way to stop it.

She reached up to beat on the glass bricks with the flashlight.

They were not window panes. They would not break under her feeble blows. No use.

She screamed. She had little breath to scream.

She tried to get to the garden door again to beat at it, to rouse the world, to make a noise. Something flooded up from within her body and overwhelmed her in a dark swift tide. She whimpered, once, softly, pitifully, like a tired baby.

The flash lay on the floor beside her. It broke as it fell. So there was darkness, and no noise. Only the gentle continuing whisper of the gas.

25.

"There go the lights," said Gene. "somebody just turned them off."

"Yeah. Hold it."

"Listen, you guys better get out and walk."

"Maybe you're right, at that. No cover down here, though."

"You'd make a hell of a noise on that hillside."

"Keep on the road, then. Take the inside. Stick to the wall."

"Yeah."

"Here goes."

They darted, one after the other, across the bare road. They stood close under Tobias' wall. They listened. Nothing.

Kelly went first. He walked very softly on the harsh ground, his feet scrabbling as little as was humanly possible. Gene came next, tiptoe and not so steady. The driver was behind. They piled up on each other behind a wild shrub.

No sound from the garage. It was there as it had been there, pushed into the hill and squat, with the half-story hump of the workshop silent on its back.

Nothing to see. Nothing to hear.

Kelly muttered impatiently and walked boldly around the

bush. He went directly to the doors of the garage and tried them. They were locked and firm. They didn't budge. He leaned his head on the painted surface. There was no sound. No car motor was running behind these doors or he was deaf all of a sudden.

His face soured in the dark. "Nah," he said.

"Maybe it's too soon." Gene's breath fluttered.

"Changed their minds, eh?" said the driver. "Nothing doing?"

"Nuts!" said Kelly. He walked off down the road toward the car. The others followed. The driver stolidly, Gene hopping.

"Listen."

Kelly stood still but he wasn't listening. Considerations of his full duty, a vague feeling of abuse, floated in his mind. "You can stick around if you want to," he said.

"I guess I—guess I will," said Gene. He felt nervous. He didn't know why. He didn't want them to go. But he could think of no reason why they should stay.

Kelly put his foot on the running board. He said broodingly, "Maybe we'll take a run back here, half hour or an hour. You'll— uh—stick around, you think?"

"Yeah," said Gene, "for a while." He swallowed.

"O.K. It's all yours."

The police car moved. It went on to the dead end of the canyon, swung around, came back, passed Gene again. The headlights went on as it proceeded, more nimbly now, toward the canyon mouth.

"What d'ya say?" asked the driver.

"Nuts!" said El Kelly. "I'm going to get hold of those kids tomorrow, both of them, and see what the hell they thought was going to happen."

"Didn't happen," said the driver cheerfully.

"Nah," said El Kelly. "Whatever it was they expected, they had it figured wrong."

Gene stood on one foot. He wished he could telephone. He thought maybe he could sneak up on the hill the front way and peek in the windows. Then he thought no, he'd better not. Better stick around. This was where she'd said to be. He went back to the sycamore. He thought, Darn her hide! When I get hold of her . . . Her and her cops and robbers!

In the big studio, above, the four of them were grouped around the fire.

Ione, in her sofa corner, had taken up her knitting. Her fingers were busy. Her little feet swung from time to time as she would glance over the spectacles that looked so delightfully absurd on her cute little nose. She would glance at Tobias. She seemed to watch him, covertly.

He was not drinking his milk. The new glass rested on the arm of his chair with his hand around it. He seemed to have forgotten it. Well, she would not remind him. For he would need it, most desperately, a little later.

She nodded to herself. She went on knitting, placidly.

Fanny was rigid. Her voice tumbled on. She was telling some rambling tale. It went on without her attention, like a phonograph record she'd set under the needle. Her shrewd eyes were well aware of Thone. She didn't understand, but she loved him. So she held in abeyance, in tight control, the growing fright she felt. The doubt, wonder, the blend of memory and shock, the hideous impossible suspicions. She watched him covertly. He was so tense, as if he were waiting!

She forced herself not to hear her own question. What—oh, what!—was Thone waiting for?

Tobias lay in the chair. He felt that if he tried, he could not lift his head. He could not lift his hand, with the glass. He would never move again. He was undermined, his strength all drained out. His head was turned enough, as it lay, to see the liqueur glass near Thone's right hand. Thone had not taken any of it. Not yet.

Tobias would not move until he did. Until there was proof. . . . He was weak . . . weak. . . . He had no faith and no strength to reach for any. He needed—God pity his doubt!—to see Thone drink that stuff. He needed to see that when he did so, nothing would happen.

He wished the boy would drink, would move and release him. He could not speak to suggest. . . . He lay in the chair.

Thone thought, She's called it off. What happened?

He thought, If nothing's happened, if Mandy just went down and took the car and is now halfway to Inglewood after those damned fuchsias—then what? Will it be later, when she comes back? No, for God's sake. The drug would have worked in ten or fifteen minutes. It's not going to wait two or three hours. Never. And Ione would know that.

Whatever she had planned to do—and she had tried to drug Mandy—it must be now. It should have been before now!

For all she knew, Mandy was unconscious down there, right now, this minute. And she sat knitting!

Well, then, maybe she'd had the car running all afternoon. If that was possible. But Gene would have heard it. And Mandy herself, of course, would have heard it, and known. They'd make a move soon. They'd come in. Perhaps with Kelly.

Perhaps any minute. They'd all walk in with the thing sewed up. Explained. And over.

Meanwhile, Ione was knitting. He watched the yarn slip on the fingers.

She couldn't have had the car running all day. But she was down there this morning and only this morning!

Still, what other way . . . ?

But why didn't they come?

No, she must have called the whole thing off. And Mandy and Gene had so decided and Gene had probably ridden along to the airport.

But if she'd called it off, something had alarmed her. Maybe he hadn't fooled her. Maybe he'd interrupted when he'd met her there below this morning.

But, if so, why the dose of chloral?

No, up to then, it had been cooking all right.

Had he scared her off, just now, in the kitchen? Had he, by impatience, mere childish impatience, stopped her then, at the last minute, from going out, from going on with it? Had she thought she'd better not? Had the moment passed?

Many moments were passing.

But, if so, then she must believe that Mandy lay unconscious. Or—his heart jumped—had she somehow slipped out before he'd got to the kitchen at all, and . . .

No, no. All was well. Because Gene was down there. And Mandy hadn't had the drug, of course, and wasn't going to be knocked out at all, and therefore . . .

But why didn't they come? Or call? Or somehow let him know? He ground his teeth. Suppose Gene hadn't made it? And Kelly got no note? And Mandy had fallen and hurt herself. She must have walked in a fog of terror. He conquered and reined in the skittish flight of his thought down wild improbable alleys.

Ione had called it off and Mandy was quite safe and bewildered, and had gone on the errand, not daring to communicate with him. How could she, after all? So uncertain, not knowing what to do except follow the path of normal action, she'd been forced to leave his fear dangling alive, although she knew, now, that it was unnecessary.

Still, she could phone.

Or they were having trouble with Kelly. Yes, it could be that. An argument, or a long confab, in which they were consolidating what each of them knew into one full story.

But time beat past! Too much time! It was taking too long!

He moved convulsively, and to cover it, picked up the glass of liqueur. Automatically, it began to rise to his lips. He had forgotten what was in it.

Tobias' body heaved in the chair. "No, Thone. No, son. Don't . . ."

Thone turned at the cry. He read the truth on his father's anguished face.

"Forgive . . ." Tobias read the look he got. Was this, then, the right glass? "Forgive me the doubt, my son." Then, in an utterly different and terrible fear, he whispered, "Go ahead, drink it. Why don't you drink it!" The whites of his eyes ringed his pupils all around. He stretched out his hand, pleading with fact to be otherwise. Milk spilled for the second time.

Thone cried, "Ah, Dad," in terrible reproach. He threw away

the crutch. The sweep and thrust of his arms brushed glasses off the table. His body surged up. If there was pain to his damaged foot as he ran from the room he did not feel any.

Ione stood up, trembling.

"Look out! Toby!" cried Fanny. "Oh, Toby—look!"

Ione looked. Tobias lay as if he had died. His white head slumped off the chair arm. His limp hand pointed down at the mess on the carpet.

26.

Thone went down the stairs as if he were sliding. On the lowest floor he checked himself. He opened the door to Mandy's room, in hope, but one glance told him she was not there. He did not call to her. He knew, now, that wherever she was, she would not hear.

He bellowed back up the core of the house, "Turn on the floodlights." He ran down the hall to the door that led outside. He knew he must follow the way she had taken until he found her. He came out into darkness, but he had not gone far when the lights came on. Now he could search the whole lit slope with his eyes. If she had fallen anywhere in the gardens he should be able to see her from this highest shelf.

He saw no trace of her. No human heap was lying among the leaves and flowers.

Inside the garage, then. He cursed. He had no key. Then he remembered. The door was inside out. Because it was the door to his father's fortress, it locked in the opposite way. From inside the wall, he would need no key. And the middle door was never locked. He slipped and fell and rolled, clutching at plants that would not hold his plunging weight.

He sobbed, "Mandy," because he could not help it.

A man's voice was shouting, beyond the wall. "Who is it? Who is it?"

"Where's Mandy?"

"Mandy!" He heard blows on hollow wood. The noise bounced on the canyon walls. "Can't—get—in." He heard running feet and then kicking and scratching on the wall.

He picked himself up and fell against the workshop door. It opened docilely. An odor poured out.

And there she was.

Gene had scrambled, somehow, over the wall and was shouting frantically beside him. Thone prayed out loud. "It's not too late. It's not too late."

She was quite limp in his arms. He felt tireless. Gene had no chance. Gene's cries in his ears were meaningless. Alone, he carried her as if she weighed nothing, well away from that place, high up to a grassy spot where the air was pure. To Gene, who stumbled, cursing, after, he said curtly, "Shut up. Get a doctor."

"I've called a doctor," said Fanny. She was there in her black satin, with her diamonds blazing.

Thone knelt on the ground.

"If she's dead, I'll kill you," sobbed Gene Noyes.

"But she isn't," said Thone.

The time, which had seemed so long, had not been too long, after all.

"Thone," said Fanny gently, in a moment, in the silence that thickened and deepened after frantic sound, "your father has had a stroke."

He flung up his head. "I'm glad to hear it," he said bitterly.

He picked up Mandy, brushing the other man out of his way as he did so. He carried her slowly and carefully now, and gently, up toward the house. His body was suddenly a mass of aches and pains. His foot was aflame. One arm was torn and raw. But still her weight was nothing and the pain was good. Fiercely, he welcomed it.

Fanny stared after them, at the redheaded boy, whose coat was torn, who was dodging ahead to open the way. At Thone's tall figure, going steadily and somehow penitently upward. At the soft mop of Mandy's hair on his right arm, the red skirt caught up in his left, her pretty feet dangling, one slipper lost. The old actress's eyes were tortured. Her mouth curled and trembled. Her thin hand clawed at her throat.

27.

Sirens screamed up the mountain. The ambulance came, with oxygen. Soon El Kelly's car came screaming and pelting after. At the back, lights blazed, forgotten, over the terraces. At the front, cars parked crookedly and curious folk came out of the hills and stood in the road.

A little later came Kate Garth in her Chevrolet. Gene had gone to the telephone, saying angrily that he trusted no one of them in that place. So Kate came in, past the cop at the door, like a wind blowing under his chin. She came for her child.

They had taken Tobias to his own bed. An intern from the ambulance was with him. A nurse was coming. He was not conscious. He did not, for now, need even the nurse. But Thone had insisted. Thone had lashed about him with command. So Tobias lay, unconscious and professionally attended, and there was nothing for Ione to do.

Mandy lay on the couch in the studio with her eyes open. She'd had oxygen and intravenous infusions and injections and what not. She was covered warmly now. There was no hubbub.

The room was hushed to reverent quiet. Kate's panic and anger ran slam into this artificial peace.

So she went quietly and put her strong hand over Mandy's limp paws. A weak tear slid out of Mandy's eye. Kate kissed her and hushed her and sat by. The doctor spoke in hushed tones to the mother. He was pleased, he said, with the action of the pulse. A fine strong girl. Kate said nothing, and although she drew her breath again more freely, her arm, braced back of Mandy's body, was like iron.

The canyon house was a hospital.

Ione sat on the window seat, alone, silently. From time to time she put a dainty handkerchief to her lips and eyes.

Fanny huddled in a chair and watched everything with brilliant, feverish eyes. Her hands twisted her bracelets, round and round.

Thone sat, back bent in weary reaction, head in his hands. Gene had gone out of the room and walked restlessly up and down, up and down, noiselessly on the hall carpet.

El Kelly talked with his men, with Gene, with Burt and Elsie, who came blinking into the strange hushed tumult. All these low voices hummed, softly, afar, in the dining room. Now and again there were feet on the stairs. Men prowled in the gardens. For a while the people in the road murmured. Then they drifted homeward.

A little life crept back to the house. Mandy stirred and sat up a little higher. El Kelly came in from across the hall. "Feeling better, Miss Garth?"

"Much, much better."

"I'd like to try to make a little sense out of this. How about it?" He looked to the doctor.

"Quietly," the doctor said. "No excitement."

Kelly ran his hand through his hair. "I'm going to need this girl. You tell me if she should talk now."

"Quietly," the doctor said, frowning. He stood by.

"I've been talking to young Noyes and the servants." Kelly sat down, speaking conversationally. "My men have been looking around, one place and another. As far as I can see, this could have been an accident caused, in part, by the fact that you kids," he coupled Thone and Amanda with his glance, "were all hot and bothered about a plot. The gas pipe down there is out of whack. The gardener tells me that he may have done that when he was digging at its point of entry outside, just today. All right. So, as I see it, you kids are all worked up. She—Amanda—goes down there, scared to death before she starts. Gets inside the door. Smells gas. Goes into a panic. The key comes off the case and gets kicked around. And so . . ." He shrugged.

Mandy's lips parted.

"Don't you talk yet," El Kelly told her. "Lemme plow through some of the rest of this first. You listen and let nothing worry you. All that's going to happen is, I'll find out the truth."

The doctor said, "But she was drugged."

"Yeah?" El Kelly chewed some nonexistent gum. "Well, let's see. Garrison, suppose you tell me what happened. Make it short."

"My stepmother tried to kill her." Thone spoke through his fingers, hands still over his face. "She dosed Amanda's drink with chloral."

"How do you know?"

"I saw her do it. So I changed Amanda's glass for mine. But my father changed them back." His voice was quite monotonous. "I don't know how she worked the rest of it."

From the window seat Ione gasped and straightened her back.

"The motive?" asked Kelly calmly. "Why?"

"Because she hated and murdered my mother," said Thone, "six years ago. And she thought Amanda was my mother's child."

"What made her think that?" Kelly's brows went up in astonishment. Ione, on the window seat, did not move. Fanny was white-faced with shock.

Kate said, in a moment, "Amanda is my child."

"Everybody knew that," Thone dropped his hands at last, "except Ione." He didn't look at her.

Ione said, "No . . . no." Her hands wrenched at the amethyst beads.

Kelly didn't look at her, either. "Cockeyed motive," he mused. "So you think she fixed the doors. Locked the one. Left the other so it would open, I guess, huh, and then lock itself? How would she know the key would fall off?"

"It wasn't on," said Amanda firmly. The doctor caught her wrist. She said no more.

El Kelly looked startled. "Uh-huh," he said. "So I'm changing my mind. We've got an attempted murder here. What do you know about it, Miss Austin?"

Fanny said through chattering teeth, "I'll tell you all I know. It's the only way. What Thone says about his stepmother, I—I can't speak about. I do know the girl tried to make herself out

Belle's child. It's a funny story." Her graceful hand turned at the wrist, despairing of telling that story now. "As for this evening, they were drinking Herbsaint. Belle's drink. I saw Thone change his glass for hers. That's true. I don't know—don't know—any more." Fanny shook her hennaed head. Her bracelets tinkled.

Kelly frowned at the stained carpet. His men had what they could gather up of the mess that they'd found there. "She got chloral, did she, Doctor?"

"Oh, yes. Yes, certainly. Not a dangerous dose, I believe. But I took all precautions."

"Chloral again."

"I did get it," murmured Mandy, "after all! I passed right out."

Kelly was very quick. "After all, eh? You thought she was going to give it to you? But you thought he—this, uh, Thone—was going to change the glasses. That was part of the plot, eh?" He forgot to hush her.

She said, "Yes. I thought he had." Kate's hands were at her shoulders to persuade her to rest.

Kelly looked at the others. "Anybody else see the old man change them back?" No one said anything. "But you saw it, Garrison?"

"My God, no," said Thone. "I let her drink it!"

Gene, sitting tensely, to Kelly's rear, bared his teeth.

"How do you know he changed them back, then? Did he say so? Anybody hear him say so?" No one spoke. "Guessing, eh?" said Kelly. "Can we ask the old man, Doc?"

"Not now." The doctor shrugged. "Maybe never."

There was a faint sobbing sound from Ione, where she sat

apart. El Kelly turned his body in the chair. "Well, Mrs. Garrison, let's start with the poison in the chocolate. What do you say?"

"I beg your pardon?" She stopped grief with surprise.

"There was poison in the chocolate," said Gene Noyes hoarsely.

"Can you tell us who put it there?" said Kelly without turning his head. Gene licked his lips.

"I have no idea what you mean," said Ione in the blankest of tones.

El Kelly moved his shoulders. "All right. Skip that for now. Tell me your version of tonight. Go ahead."

Ione got up and came on her little feet, toward them. She took the edge of the armless chair, bending her little body forward a trifle, sitting alert and yet decorously. "Of course. I will try to help you, Lieutenant." Her eyes rolled as if she gathered and organized her thoughts. She began to speak quietly but precisely. "This Amanda Garth came here with a tale of babies in a hospital. She wanted us to believe that she was the true child of my husband and his second wife." She swept a glance around the circle and heads nodded, except Kate's.

"My husband, whatever he believed, at least grew quite fond of her. He asked her here. There was no reason why this should upset *me*, Lieutenant. But I don't think Thone . . . liked it."

She looked at Thone. Her eyes challenged him to deny it. He was sitting with his hands on the arms of his chair, feet flat on the floor. His lips parted but he did not speak.

The dark eyes went to Fanny. Fanny responded. "Naturally, he didn't want Toby upset. Also, he did think, at least at first, that she was deliberately trying to take his place because—well, he has his mother's money."

"Why, so he has," drawled Ione. Very soft and thoughtful the syllables were.

Mandy was looking at the ceiling with a little frown. Fanny said harshly, "It was just a brief notion. Later he came to believe she had some . . . delusion. . . ." She put her lips together and shook her head again.

Kate bristled, but Kelly held his hand up. "Go on," he said coldly to Ione.

"The child's very much in love with Thone, of course." The white head trembled as if in pity. But she didn't look at Mandy. She looked at Thone.

He was watching her with a grave stare. He seemed to have frozen where he sat.

Fanny said grimly, "Yes, I think so. We must all say exactly what we think. It's the only way." She turned her bracelet. Kate's eyes met hers. Some signal for boldness and some faith in it passed between them.

Kate said, deliberately, "That's true. Mandy told me. That's true and that's why—"

"Why what, Mrs. Garth?"

"Why she came here, really. Not in the hope of money." Kate's scorn was deep.

Mandy roused herself on her elbow and looked at the mask of Thone's face. "Oh, sure. That's true," she said carelessly, as if her thoughts were elsewhere.

"It seems," said Ione, wrinkling her brow, "there was some

kind of plotting going on? Between them?" she was addressing Kelly but Thone answered.

"There was. We went to Lieutenant Kelly about it. We arranged for Gene to be in the canyon, on guard."

"Yeah, Mandy called me," Gene put in nervously.

"To be on guard. For something resembling your mother's death?" asked Ione softly. Thone's face was stone. "Involving the automobile?"

Kelly wished he had a man back of this Thone's chair. He didn't like the looks of those hands. He didn't like the calm. "I knew about that," he said uneasily. "But they figured wrong."

"Did they?" said Ione. Her hands played with the amethysts. It was as if a cold wind blew in the long room.

"Proceed," said Kelly.

"I wonder . . ." said Ione. "You see," she lowered her head in a ducking motion, "I know I have nothing to do with it. So perhaps I can see rather more clearly. I am not confused."

Thone's hands gripped the chair arms.

"Oh, I'm so afraid!" Her eyes, turned sideways, watched him as if she were, indeed, afraid, and yet must speak. "I'm so afraid Thone did this thing. For his father knew it." She gasped as if emotion caught up with the mind. She clutched at her beads. "It's frightening, Mr. Kelly. It's quite—horrible, to me." Her body rocked. "But, as Fanny says, we must say all we are thinking. This is the only way."

"Proceed," said Thone hoarsely.

"So Thone did it, eh?" Kelly spoke impersonally, as if he mentioned a mere puzzle. He was trying to play down the emotional side. "His motive was jealousy, like? Afraid she was getting into his place with his father? And also that she'd get the money?"

"Yes, I suppose . . ." She sighed.

"So he pretends to plot, you mean. You're talking about a double cross."

"Am I?" said Ione. "I was only thinking, if he drugged his own glass and got her to agree that they be changed . . . That would make it so easy."

"I saw you," said Thone, "in the window glass."

"So you say." Dark eyes were insolent. "Although you are lying."

He seemed to break a little. His hands rose, trembling, in a defensive gesture. "I couldn't have doped Mandy's drink. Dad changed them back. That's how she got it."

"So you say." Her eyes glittered. "We can't ask Toby, can we?"

Kelly sat a little more upright. "Glasses and dope all mixed up," he muttered angrily. "Who is going to say which glass was which any more now?" His eyes were hard on the man. "But lemme tell you this, Garrison, before you go any further. I already know that there are fragments, identifiable fragments, of your prints and Mrs. Garrison's and the girl's on both those little liqueur glasses. But not one trace of your father's that we can find."

"He turned the table," said Thone. He spun it, now, to demonstrate how it could revolve.

"But you didn't see him do that?"

"No. I'd planned to do it that way, myself. It was bare, because I'd cleared it."

"Uh-huh." Kelly grunted. "Anybody see the table turn?" No

one answered. "Maybe you turned it yourself, after all," mused Kelly, "if this is a double cross."

Thone didn't seem to hear. He was back in his pose of terrifying control.

"Well, anyhow, it looks pretty much as if either Thone Garrison or Mrs. Ione Garrison doped the drink. No other choice." Ione opened her lips as he said this, but shut them again. It would do. It was good enough. Kelly looked at her rather oddly. "Any more?" he asked.

Ione said, "Wasn't there something about the workshop doors?"

"Yeah. The middle door was locked. Gardener says it isn't, usually. Now, I'd say it's pretty plain somebody fixed it to lock and fixed the pipe so it was leaking, on purpose, too."

"Thone was down there. On the lowest terrace. This morning. With that foot of his, imagine. Oh, dear!" Ione was breathless. She rallied. She said, "I met him there as I came in. We came up together. Of course, I don't know how long he had been there before I . . ."

"That so?"

"I didn't go into the workshop," said Thone with stiff lips. "She, however, came out of it."

"Anyone to witness that?"

"No. Burt went around the corner. Mandy was on the phone. No, I guess not." Thone slid his hands on the chair. He was thinking, she'll trip herself. She's being so clever. She'll trip herself yet.

Mandy lay with a lazy smile on her lips, scarcely seeming to follow all this.

Kelly cleared his throat. He was lying low. *He* didn't know. Let them fight it out.

"Something about the key?" asked Ione brightly.

"Yeah. We found it under a pile of junk. Amanda tells us it wasn't on the case at all. You'd say he *left* it down there?"

Ione raised her brows.

"Her key," said Thone.

"Which lies about the house all day," she sighed.

"Wait a minute, now. You say you came through that place, Mrs. Garrison, and the two of you came up together. Was there any odor of gas?"

"No." She was quite definite. "No. None at all. Ah, then it couldn't be, could it?" She seemed to relax. She even seemed to be glad.

"That gas line has a valve in the service porch," said Thone sharply. "Right up here."

"Oh, dear . . ." said Ione.

"Yeah?" Kelly peered from one to the other.

"It's true. It's true," moaned Ione, pursing her soft lips. "And while I was waiting there to turn off the lights after Amanda left . . . I'm afraid he came out. He did come out there. With his foot and all, just at that time. He said it was for a drink of water. He rather—chased me away when I tried to help. I left him there. Fanny will tell you. Oh, Lieutenant," she shrunk in her chair, letting her spine bend as if truth overwhelmed her, "how could he guess how it was done, if he hadn't done it?"

"Uh-huh."

"And another thing!" She straightened with a jerk. "Oh, when

I came out the workshop door, it wasn't locked. He'd left it—so I could come through. The key, you see. The key . . ."

Gene said, "God damn it!" glaring at Thone.

"What about *this* fellow?" said Kelly suddenly. "Let me hear you explain the fact that this fellow was called in. Why did Thone take the risk of having him hanging around?"

"So little risk, as it turned out," she murmured. "Still, it was Amanda who called him. Did Thone even know that?"

"I knew it," said Thone stupidly. Amanda's eyes widened a little.

"Or," said Ione airily, "does he only pretend, now, that he knew it?"

"I think you can see," said Thone, "how clever she is. How her mind works."

Silence fell on the long room. Fanny fingered her diamonds. Kate said, in a loud voice, "Amanda is coming home. I don't care who—"

Gene said, "Yeah, she's got to get out of here. Nobody's going to have a second chance."

"Just a minute. Just a minute," said Kelly. "This thing doesn't jell, you know. Not yet. So he fixes to kill the girl and then he gallops down there, foot and all, as you keep saying, to save her life." He looked foxy and triumphant.

"Yes," said Ione in a trembling voice. She looked down at her hands. "Oh, yes."

"Well?" said Kelly.

"It was so sly," she said. "Ugly and sly. His mother's accident gave him so many ideas. Haunting him all these years. It was easy to fool poor little Mandy. She was so blindly in love. Knowing nothing whatever about him. All ready to believe in an old murder, if he wished her to. Poor romantic child. *He* could do no wrong. How easy it must have been! What an eager little victim, walking right into it, blind with love! Oh . . ." Ione went on with passion, "I suppose he'd have called her death a suicide. A girl did kill herself, you know. Maybe you don't know. But it was for love of him. He had that precedent." The soft, prim little mouth writhed. "The precedent of his fatal charm!" she added venomously.

"Yeah, but he changed his mind," insisted Kelly.

"Ah, can't you see? Don't you remember? What happened up here?" Ione lifted the handkerchief. Her face made as if to weep at last. "My blessed Toby can't speak—or move—perhaps not even live! So of course it wasn't necessary to kill anyone. What can it matter now? His father's gone, as good as gone. He'll make no new disposal of Belle's fine money. Adopt no daughter. Why take the risk? There was no need. He *saw* that, Lieutenant. And then, of course, she's a lusty little armful! And so ripe!" Her body was vibrating, hating. She covered the malice with her handkerchief. "Oh, that all this has broken my Toby's heart," she cried through the cloth, "Thone doesn't care!"

Fanny put her old dyed head down on the chair and began to cry, brokenheartedly.

Kelly's eyes swiveled to Thone. "Well?" he said, deep in his throat, like a growl.

28.

The sounds the weeping women made grated on the nerves.

Thone said, so low he could scarcely be heard at all, "And we still don't know how . . ." He linked his fingers, elbows on the chair. He looked boldly at Kelly. "What, out of all this stuff, do *you* believe?"

Kelly said, above the womanish noise, "Nobody can hang on what I've got. Not till I fill it in. But I'll fill it in."

Gene bounced to his feet. "Mandy, you come home! The policemen can handle it. You come away from this double-crossing louse!"

"What?" said Mandy. She stirred. She pushed at the blanket. She moved her feet. Her mother's body was still in the way.

Kate said, "Mandy, darling, we're going to take you home now."

"Oh, not now," said Mandy. The other women left off weeping as she raised her head. She was dizzy, suddenly. Her face went white. She felt very rocky, trying to sit up. But she batted the doctor's hand away. Her stockinged foot, the slipperless one, nudged at Kate's haunches.

"Go home," said Thone.

Half up, she stared at him. His face was as white as hers. "Why?" she said. She could feel Kate's angry doubt and Gene's conviction, Fanny's despair, all answering why.

"Because, for all you know, she's right." Thone stated it quietly.

Color was coming back to her cheeks. Her mouth began the sweet curve of her smile. "I know more than you think," said Mandy mischievously.

Thone's face changed like magic. The mask fell off. Mandy looked away. Her heart was singing. She got her feet to the floor, kicked off her other shoe, and curled up her toes. "Boy, she sure is a wily customer," said Mandy, and grinned at the policeman. "But we can put up quite a long story, too, you know, and just as fancy."

"We . . ." Thone choked.

Mandy said with bubbling cheer. "Fanny Austin, you funny old thing. What makes you think he'd be that slimy?"

"But he was glad," mourned Fanny, "about Tobias. He was glad!"

"Shouldn't we be?" said Mandy, more soberly. "Do you think he'd enjoy these goings on?"

Fanny lifted her head.

Mandy said, "It's all very well to horse around. After all, I'm alive, so that's O.K. But what about her? What about Belle? Darn it, we didn't get it! We still don't know how . . ." Her eyes slid past Ione as if she weren't there. "Although . . . Mr. Kelly, you do believe Thone changed those glasses? Fanny's an honest witness. You can say to yourself, that's true?" The Lieutenant was forced to nod. "Now, I did get doped. You can admit that, can't you? So if only we could prove his father changed them back . . . As far as all the rest of it goes, why, she had her chance, exactly as well as

Thone, or even better. So it depends which drink I got. If I drank the one she fixed for me and the one Thone tried to keep me from getting, well? That sorts things out, wouldn't you say?"

"I guess you're right at that," said Kelly with sudden heartiness. "Any chance, Doc?"

The doctor went out to the hall. He came back looking almost nettled with surprise. "He's conscious," he said. "That is, as far as we can tell. He can't speak, you know. Whether he can hear or understand, I don't venture . . ."

"If he could answer just one question," said Amanda, vivid with hope, "it would make the difference."

"One question," said Kelly, hopeful himself. "Would it hurt to try?"

The doctor looked at Mandy rather tenderly. "If he can't be reached, can't hear, why, no harm. If he can, one question . . ." He settled his shoulders. "Perhaps, under these circumstances, it's up to his—family."

Thone looked at Ione and she at him.

"Don't—" she began and bit her lip.

"Shall we try?" said Thone. His face had thawed. It sparkled in mocking challenge.

"Oh, poor Toby," she murmured, voice distressed, eyes crafty. "But of course we must try."

As they got up to move stiffly out of this seated pattern, Mandy and Thone were wafted as if a current bore them toward each other until their shoulders touched. Gene pushed past Kate and caught Amanda's arm.

"I'm sorry, honey," he said. "You could be right. You know more about it than I do. Sorry." He glanced at Thone. "But, God

Almighty, Mandy, when I saw you lying in there and I thought there was blood all over . . ."

"Blood?" said Thone stupidly.

Mandy was looking straight into Gene's eyes. "I know," he said, "it's just one of those things. Don't tell me how fond of me you are. I know that. I know."

"But I thank you," said Mandy. Her fingers went slipping under Thone's arm and suddenly, convulsively, he squeezed them to his side.

29.

Tobias lay alive, if it could be called life. He breathed. In his room, here on the upper floor, which was vast, he lay in a double bed, sheet to his chin, arms limp outside the covering. He lay, and his eyes were open although they looked blind.

No one questioned Mandy's right to go to his bedside, to bring herself in her crimson frock, with her dirty face, her tousled hair, to a spot where, if he could see, he would see her. Thone stood close behind her. All the wires were up and vibrating between them now.

Ione was at the right of the bed. If Tobias could see, she, in her lavender, was in his sight also.

Kelly and the doctor stood a pace or two away from the foot of the bed. At the open door, Fanny peered in and Kate, unwilling to let Mandy out of her reach, was beside the actress. Gene alone remained in the hall, biting on a sense of loss, as one worries an aching tooth.

The doctor took an uncertain step forward. "Mr. Garrison . . ."

"Toby, dear . . ." said Ione musically.

He did not rouse.

"Dad . . ." said Thone. Mandy felt at her back the coursing of sudden grief through his body.

Tobias lay alive. If thoughts moved in his brain at all, they would be old patches, memories and tags, a hodge-podge. He did not seem to hear or even to know that they were there.

"I doubt if he *can* tell us . . ." the doctor began.

But Fanny spoke excitedly. "There's that old French book. What is it? Something by Dumas. The old man and the eyelids! Don't you remember? He made a sign with his eyelids! Ask . . ."

The doctor took one startled, unhappy glance at her. "Can you close your eyes, sir? If so, will you?"

The weary lids trembled. They did tremble.

"I'll ask it," Kelly moved closer. "Mr. Garrison," he said in a quiet, respectful, and somehow official voice, "if you turned the table in the other room and changed the glasses around, will you please close your eyes."

Tobias lay with his eyes open. If he heard, they couldn't tell.

"If you did *not*," said Kelly desperately, "will you try to tell us so. By closing your eyes."

The sick old man kept staring. He did not even blink. If his mind took in impressions, they could not tell. Nothing reacted. Nothing returned.

"Ah, maybe he can't . . ." cried Mandy. Her heart filled up with pity and love. She sat on the bed and took his poor hand. She smiled her loveliest. The eyes seemed to rest on her face. Then, slowly, they closed.

Thone turned to look at the Lieutenant.

Ione said tremulously, "Come away. That's enough. Oh, come away."

But Mandy bent down and kissed the quiet hand that would paint no more. She didn't believe he had answered anything. She brooded, watching his face. Behind her, someone's breath sawed painfully.

In a moment, Tobias reopened his eyes. She thought she saw the tiniest flicker of an expression. Thone thought so, too. He leaned. "Dad . . ."

Something about the eyes said, No. No, you shall not rouse me. No, I will not come back. No, it's too much to bear. I cannot. I will not. Let me go.

Mandy stifled the need to sob. She thought, he's going to die and he'll never know. He's got that burden, that awful burden. He thinks Belle killed herself. He still thinks so. He has no doubt. If we could only tell him it wasn't so. If it were only proved so that we could tell him for sure.

The room seemed to have fallen under a spell. It settled as it was. They were like statues, grouped, waiting. Waiting on death, perhaps. In the upper spaces of the chamber it poised its black wings. Ione's back was straight. Her little pigeon bosom swelled under the lavender silk. She folded her hands, to wait with courage and decorum. The folding of those small hands was a kind of victory. Minutes passed.

Mandy's glance caught a catalogue lying on the bedside table. A catalogue of Tobias' recent show. It was folded to a black and white reproduction of "Belle in the Doorway." She thought, Dare I lift it up? If I should hold it up, could he see? Dare I even try to remind him of Belle now? Her heart, her pity answered, No. Idly, her eye traced the lines of the work. Such a stupid . . . !

She caught at this trace of an old thought in surprise. That was what she'd thought when she saw it in the newspaper, when she'd first seen it, the day Cousin Edna had left. That Sunday morning, eons ago. Wait. Why stupid? Why had she been so harsh and even brutal in her judgment and then, when she'd seen the picture itself, gone overboard in plunging excitement and admiration?

She turned her mind in on itself, examining some movement of thought that had been continuing without her conscious attention. All this time, she realized, there had been a word beating in her brain. Blood? Blood? Blood?

She caught at that, too. Where had it come from? That word, in that tone. Why, Thone had said it, as she kept hearing it, in dull surprise, in total blank incomprehension. As if he said, "Blood? Why blood?" Gene, of course, had meant her red dress. That's what he'd seen on the workshop floor. But Thone . . . He knew, of course. He expected her red dress. Yet he didn't understand.

Her mind began to race, clicking off one point after another. She got to her feet, trembling.

"Thone," she said, very quietly. It didn't matter that Tobias lay there. He would not hear. Nerve failed her and she hedged. "Have you a driver's license?" she faltered.

"I wangled one," he murmured, barely attending. "I shouldn't have it."

She knew why not! She knew why he'd had trouble getting the Army to take him. Why he'd had to talk his way through the war. And why he'd let her drive the car. And why he'd mistaken, that same day, her yellow and dark blue costume for the yellow and brown she'd worn before. Why he'd seen no difference! Why he wasn't a painter! Although he understood line and space. Why he'd seen nothing to make him think of blood, as she lay in her crimson on the floor!

"You are color-blind," she said aloud, "aren't you?"

"Yes. Of course."

The doctor squirmed. But nothing disturbed Tobias. Nothing could touch him. Somehow, they were all listening to Mandy and she went on.

"Your mother was color-blind, too," she said.

"She was, yes." Thone's attention caught up with the conversation. "Why, Mandy?"

"It's unusual in women." She was so excited she could hardly stand.

"Very. But she was."

Oh, yes, of course Belle was color-blind. Witness the drab and neutral clothes she wore until she met Tobias, that colorist, that man in love with the rainbow. And afterward, how she'd never dared vary her "costumes," as Fanny said. Of course, she wore what the dressmaker put together, since this only was guaranteed against clashing error. Oh, no, Belle didn't care for painting. Could not. And of course she rarely drove a car: she had no license.

"Why didn't you say!" Mandy's voice raised a little. "Oh, Thone, Thone, why didn't you ever say!"

"She was a little bit sensitive about it," said Thone, quietly, matter-of-fact. "She never spoke of it. So we didn't, either."

Just quietly, like that, they never spoke of it.

"But that's why she didn't like the picture!" cried Mandy, "and you don't, either. 'Belle in the Doorway'! I don't like it, myself, without the color!"

"It's . . . No . . ." He was letting her lead him. He knew she was going somewhere. He didn't know where.

Amanda said, "Mr. Kelly, about the Consolidated Cab Company. What's painted on those cabs? Do you know?"

"The name," said Kelly in astonishment. "Why?"

"Not the *color*?"

"Huh?"

"Not the word 'green'?"

"No."

"Did you tell your mother, the night she died," she cried at Thone, "that her cab, when it came, would be green?"

"I never even knew. Anyhow, why would I tell her? It wouldn't have meant anything to her. She couldn't . . ."

"Ah, but she did! The woman in the road!" Mandy turned on Ione. "*You* did! Out there in the road, that night. You could tell. And you didn't know Belle was color-blind, did you? Or you'd never have called out, 'Cab . . . green cab.'"

"Wait a minute," said Kelly. "That driver positively identified Mrs. Garrison."

"He was mistaken," said Mandy. "He was just plumb wrong. This Mrs. Garrison, yes. But not Belle. Not possibly Belle. Not Belle at all.

"And that's how she did it. *She* sent the cab away. She took Belle with her, somehow. That's how she got her chance to murder Belle. Nobody mixed up chloral in this house. She must have . . ."

"My patient," said the doctor crisply. "All of you, please. Get out of this room."

But Mandy bent down. She said to the living eyes, "She murdered Belle. She tried to murder me. You'll help us prove that, now. You did change the glasses? Close your lids, say yes."

Tobias closed his eyelids. It was perfectly deliberate. It had meaning. The eyes that opened again were alive.

"Oh, dear . . . dear . . ." sobbed Mandy. "No, no, she never meant to leave you. She never would have gone. Now you can be sure."

"Oh, no," cried Thone in pain, "never would she leave you! Ah, Dad, why didn't you tell me, why did you keep it from me, what you thought? I could have told you."

"This will not do!" snapped the doctor.

But Mandy, as they collected themselves and rose, thought privately that it did very well.

Something about Tobias was at peace.

Not once did he glance at Ione.

Kelly's grasp was on that little lady's arm. She let him draw her away. There was nothing in here that belonged to her. All here was Belle's.

30.

Hubbub rose in the studio. Fanny was wild. Gene was asking questions and she declaimed the answers as they came to her. Her fury rose with her understanding. Kate followed the story, exclaiming her horror, as Fanny worked it out. How Ione could have taken the spare keys from the drawer, the whole hideous design. Kelly listened and helped speculate aloud about the blue scarf around Belle's neck and how it had got there. How she could get chloral without a prescription. A determined woman . . .

But Thone and Mandy moved silently, side by side, away from the others, down the long room to the far end. Mandy raised her eyes to the folds of concealing drapery. Thone pulled the cord that caused the folds to part and show "Belle in the Doorway." There she was, in all the glow and rapture of the artist's adoration. Thone climbed up to take it off the wall and Mandy was unsurprised. She said, agreeing, knowing what he meant to do, "Yes, he'll want to look at it now."

Thone went alone to carry it back into his father's room.

Mandy skirted the group. She walked past Ione, who was sitting in the armless chair, where she had sat before, who was silent with her hands clasped in her lap and her head bent, as she looked down and did not seem to listen to the wild and bitter words that flew around her.

Mandy climbed into a chair, sitting on her stockinged feet, resting her head on the wing. She felt as if she'd been walking and talking and living in a spotlight, on view, center stage, for a long, long, time. And now, at last, her turn was over. The time had come for her to creep off to the wings, to a quiet corner, and be still.

The enormity of her whole performance, the brassiness, the aggressiveness of it, now overwhelmed her. She felt ashamed. She blushed for her temerity. How could she meet Thone's eye when he returned? She had shouted the state of her heart to him and the whole world. She had even claimed boldly to believe he loved her. How had she dared say such a thing! What had she said and done! Now that the pressure on her was relieved, she could scarcely understand how it had seemed necessary or even possible to come with such flaming purpose into this house. What had sustained her, the fright that had been pushing her into such a role, she was already forgetting in a flood of belated shyness.

El Kelly was not entirely comfortable. He kept, even as he maintained his share in the excited talk, taking little glances at this woman who sat there so quietly, with her soft little hands folded on the lavender lap. He couldn't help but visualize that neat white head, that rosy little face, that soft rounded bosom, in a courtroom. An inner groaning followed his vision. No pair of nylon legs in the world could call up such powerful sympathy as a dear little old lady, a sweet-faced, clean, white-haired old lady, all fragrant with folk reverence, with the undefeatable power of nostalgia on her side. Everybody had a grandmother! Take the smell of ginger cookies. That was his own association, just when he looked at her.

What chance did the law have, did logic or justice or reason or probability or anything have, against the loved, lost smell of ginger cookies!

Nor was she going to break. It didn't look like it. Never would that soft clean hair come down out of the pins and be disheveled. Or that spine slump and cringe. Or the cute little face contort, haglike. Or those little hands lose the firm serenity of then present pose. Those velvet paws unsheath cruel purpose. At least, not yet.

He clicked his tongue. The voices hushed, as though, if he'd thought of something, they waited to hear what it was.

Then Ione said, "Everyone's against me." It was not a whine. It was more like a challenge. As if she read his mind, she added, "I think there will be some difficulty."

Fanny cried, "Ah, no! Not so! Lieutenant!"

Kelly chewed on his lip.

Thone had come back. He stood looking down at her now. Looming very large and tall, strangely poised and calm and unroiled by all that had happened.

"There can't be!" Fanny beat her fists together. "Belle . . . It *is* proved! Isn't it!"

"Well," said Kelly, "Belle wasn't the woman in the road. We *might* prove that much." He thought to himself it was doubtful. The cab driver had quoted the word "green" in his first interview with the police. It was on that paper in the files. But he hadn't repeated it at the inquest. Couldn't have. These people would have spotted it then, the father and the son. So how would the cab driver swear, how would he quote himself, now, six years later?

"Even if we prove it wasn't Belle, we don't prove the positive." Thone spoke without apparent anxiety. "Not to the legal mind can we prove it was Ione. Although we know."

"At least we can prove she tried to kill Mandy!"

"We know," said Kelly gloomily.

"Toby told us!"

"He's a sick man. And eyelids . . . what I mean . . ."

"God's grief!" cried Fanny. "You'll arrest her, won't you? You're not going to let her get off!"

"Sure, sure, I'll take her in. Probably stand trial."

Ione smoothed her skirt with one little hand. "I must have my glasses," she said. "And my knitting, Lieutenant?"

Kelly groaned inside.

Thone came and sat down. He stretched out his legs as if he wearily relaxed the muscles after long strain. "It doesn't really matter," he said easily.

"Not matter!" Fanny was athirst for revenge. Fanny was outraged.

But Mandy lay low. Her heart throbbed with an increasing foreboding. She held her breath, watching Thone.

"Why, no," said Thone. "Do you think the only punishment is jail?"

Ione's head tilted.

"If there is a trial," said Thone, "it will be a nasty one. Not very pleasant for any of us."

Kelly started to speak but changed his mind. Thone smiled with sudden sweetness at Kate. "Anyone in your family color-blind?"

"Mine! No, indeed not." Kate looked as if he'd accused her of something foul.

"It comes through the female. But just for fun, was your husband color-blind?"

"Heavens, no."

"So we could have proved at any minute, and beyond a doubt, whose child is whose. Since I could not be yours." He looked at Ione. His face was lit with some mocking, taunting touch of triumph, subtle and sly. "I shan't stand trial," he said. "Not me. Not Belle's child."

She folded her lips inward.

"She has her reward," said Thone to the rest, almost joyfully. "What's her life worth? Or even her freedom? She's been made a fool of, and she's failed."

Ione's mouth went slack again. She stared straight before her. The hands were still.

"Mandy fooled her. I fooled her. She put a lot of time and effort against the wrong child, and failed, at that. Even the wrong child's still alive." Thone chuckled. "And Belle! Why, Belle's all around us. Not in her grave, at all. Can't you feel it? She's here, in this house, just as radiant as in her doorway. She's with my father."

Ione moved her brow as if to say, What of that?

"This poor little thing," said Thone, and his voice went down almost to a whisper. "Look at those small hands, small as her soul. That tried to hold and squeeze and own—like a car, like a house, like a toy—another soul. So little she knows. . . . So little she understands. . . . She doesn't even know, now, that what she tried to do can't be done. Belle always knew that. She, never. Why, she was doomed to fail from the beginning. In the whole scheme of the world, which she so pitifully misunderstands, she had to fail."

"I didn't fail," said Ione shrilly. "I had him back, for years. Six years."

"Oh, no," said Thone sharply.

"Oh, yes!" Her hand curled in, grasping. "I got rid of her, I tell you! I got her out of my house! Didn't I? I tell you, she's dead! I left her on the floor! I—"

"—failed," said Thone, and sagged. "Lieutenant . . ."

"Thanks a lot," said El Kelly. "Thanks very much. That's going to help. Hey, Joe, you get that down?"

Ione stood up. She looked wildly about her. Her eyes were sick, and then they were crafty once more. "My knitting . . ." she mumbled. "My pretty yarn . . . The worms . . . The flowers will be very gay this spring. They will not stay in the flower beds. They will stroll in the garden. Nothing will stay in its grave this spring. Sunday is Easter. I must have violets. . . ." She pulled off one amethyst earring and threw it, violently.

It stung Amanda's cheek. Both Kelly and the doctor went into action.

31.

At dawn, Tobias closed his tired eyes, which had gazed sometimes with sight, sometimes without, at his masterpiece. Belle
from her doorway looked down while he died. He would never
finish Amanda in her satin.

Mandy thought her heart would break. Thone's face was so
drawn, so tired, and so luminous with his love for the departing
spirit of his father. She sobbed in Kate's arms.

"We had better go home," murmured Kate for the hundredth
time. "Won't you come now, Mandy? It's been all night long.
Honey, it's morning."

No time for love, thought Mandy. Someday. But not now. She
sobbed, "Oh, Mother, yes. Let's go home. Fanny is here. He'll
want to be quiet and she'll know . . ."

The sober duties that follow death were in train already.

Thone came to them as he sensed their decision to leave. They,
all three, moved, without speech, out of doors and stood in the
courtyard. The morning had a bloom on it, like a dark plum. Soft
haze veiled it all, the mountains, the folds and creases in their
flanks, the habitations of men and man's geometrically straight
lines and squares drawn on the land below. The air held a promise

of warmth but was yet cool and sweet.

Thone looked down at the girl's wan, tear-marked face. He smiled. He said teasingly, "You needn't think, just because you're exactly as old as I am, that I won't be the boss in the family."

"Wh-what!"

"I want the wedding," he said to Kate—to Kate!—"just as soon as it's legally possible."

Kate's long face was comical with amazement.

"And speaking of gaining a son," said Thone, "you're getting twins." He laughed and kissed Kate. And Kate—Kate!—began to cry and put her arm around his neck and smacked him, hard, on the cheek, and went out the gate to the car, bawling like a baby.

Mandy reeled and he caught her. "This is no time . . ." she stammered.

"Oh, isn't it?" The gay, sweet look went off his face, but the gravity that succeeded was as sweet and endearing. She put her hands on his lapels and looked up with utter trust, waiting for him to speak.

"Dad's death was—kind of holy, Mandy. . . ."

"Yes," she sobbed.

"She really was there, with him."

"Belle? Oh, Thone . . ."

"He had no time—to think about Ione."

"No . . . no."

"And I drank no chocolate, because you came." She clung to him. "So, it's sad, it hurts—but . . ."

"He wasn't hurt—so much," she whispered. "No, no he wasn't."

"Help me think so?" His eyes were clear, clear and blue. Then they wrinkled at the corners, softening, smiling. "What do you think love's for?" he asked.

She leaned against him, her whole body sighing. He held her lightly. His lips were on her hair.

"For a time of trouble. For now. For always," she murmured. Now is the time for love, her thought repeated with utter conviction.

"Besides," words rushed against her temple, "I have to tell you—I've got such a lot to tell you. What an absolute darling—Amanda Garth—Can't let you go. . . ."

"There's plenty of time," said Mandy. "There's years. There's now."

THE END

DISCUSSION QUESTIONS

- Amanda deceives the Garrisons in order to save Thone's life. Did you approve of this manipulation?

- What did you make of Amanda's motives for becoming involved in the Garrison family's drama?

- Were there aspects of the plot that dated the story?

- Would the story be different if it were set in the present day?

- Did the Los Angeles setting have a noticeable influence on the story? If so, how?

- Pharmaceuticals play a large role in the text. Was this emphasis featured as cultural commentary, or simply out of narrative necessity?

- What role did clothing and fashion play in the story?

- Could you imagine a different plan to catch the killer, or was Amanda's scheme the best possible method?

- Which character did you sympathize with the most?

- What did you make of the form of the narrative? Did you feel that knowing Ione's guilt from the outset made things more suspenseful?

AMERICAN MYSTERY CLASSICS

from

Available now
in hardcover and paperback:

Charlotte Armstrong . . . . *The Unsuspected*

Anthony Boucher. . . . . *Rocket to the Morgue*

John Dickson Carr . . . . *The Crooked Hinge*

Erle Stanley Gardner . . . . *The Case of the Careless Kitten*

H.F. Heard. . . . . *A Taste for Honey*

Dorothy B. Hughes . . . . *The So Blue Marble*

Frances & Richard Lockridge. . . . . *Death on the Aisle*

Stuart Palmer . . . . *The Puzzle of the Happy Hooligan*

Ellery Queen . . . . *The Dutch Shoe Mystery*

Ellery Queen . . . . *The Chinese Orange Mystery*

Patrick Quentin . . . . *A Puzzle for Fools*

Clayton Rawson. . . . . *Death From a Top Hat*

Craig Rice . . . . *Home Sweet Homicide*

Mary Roberts Rinehart. . . . . *Miss Pinkerton*

Cornell Woolrich . . . . *Waltz into Darkness*

Visit penzlerpublishers.com, email info@penzlerpublishers.com for
more information, or find us on social media at @penzlerpub